NIGHTMARES UNBOUND

Also by Harry Carpenter

FUBAR SERIES

Blackout
Out of Element
Situation Normal

Serial Killer Fiction

Memoirs of a Crazed Mind
Chemical Burns

Short Horror Story Collections

Spooky Tales and Scary Things
Spooky Tales and Scary Things 2
Spooky Tales and Scary Things 3

Harry Carpenter's

NIGHTMARES UNBOUND

Dedicated to friends, family and loved ones. My favorite thing to do is to write you into my books! The added bonus is getting to dispatch some of you.

Special thanks to my wife, Audrey, for putting up with another stupid book idea.

INTRODUCTION

In *Nightmares Unbound*, the boundaries between my life and fiction dissolve into a captivating adventure, a fantastic journey where the familiar feels strangely unreal and where the fantastical feels strikingly real. The experience is thrilling and unforgettable, a symphony of excitement that leaves you breathless and wanting more. I did this in the past with *FUBAR*, having living friends and fellow soldiers as the main ensemble. This was such a fun project for me to undertake, that I absolutely was over the moon for the second foray into a real-world bleed over book.

Dante's *Divine Comedy* was a major source of inspiration for me. One thing Dante did, for its time, was revolutionary; he'd add himself into the book from his perspective. Sure, Stephen King is essentially the guy laid up in *Misery*, but it wasn't actually King. This was an entirely different beast. Rather than have a situation inspire him, Dante wrote himself in as the protagonist and included all his "friends" into the story—people whom he looked up to, or down upon, depending on who they were. Politicians, poets, and monarchs were all found in the pages of his story. I absolutely love the ability to fictionalize myself into another story. While Chantry from *FUBAR* was basically me, this one is absolutely me.

I stared at my phone screen. I viewed the same shorthand note a million times over, until my eyes ached. *A comic con that kills everyone*—that's all it read. I didn't have a "why" or "how," but I knew my endgame. What does that look like, though? Dealing with the various intricacies of *FUBAR* was difficult enough, but the potential for the monster situation to become public knowledge added another layer of difficulty. Several of my former sergeants said the lack of leadership was unbelievable. Well, if you read the book, you find out where they went. I went through a lot of the same things with this book.

First off, how the hell does someone lure a bunch of people into an event and kill them en-masse? Second, how do they host a very public event and still do that first step and get away with it? I questioned everything as I laid down some of my scenes and plots. I set the story in Maryland but not anywhere specific. It's assumed it's at a big-city convention center, so you do the math. The traffic patterns in the city alone would cause a hell of a problem.

I decided not to opt for a known place, like the Baltimore Convention Center or any of the major hotels. I wanted a newly built place. How else could they pull all this off if some secret investor wasn't making special modifications to the building? Once I sorted out the location, I was on to the cast of characters.

The cast was always me and author Brian Paone. He was a patrolman for nearly two decades and is now a detective, and I'm former military. What would happen if a crisis happened around us? Well, we've talked about it and have even been involved in some together at conventions. We'd snap right into action. Our training comes back to us. We immediately decided we'd be leading and would try to defend survivors. My wife hates this idea because she thinks I cannot do these skills or something, yet I have proven it time and time again. I think I'd handle myself like I did in the story!

Guess what? I'm alive, spoiler alert! Shocker, right? Who else could narrate the tale? This was the hardest part for me because, like in *FUBAR*, I had to kill off friends—a decision that weighed heavily on my soul, each life lost sitting with me. While it's fun in ways, it's also disturbing and requires a certain level of darkness. When I mentioned this idea to several author and artist friends, they said, "Sign me up, fam." I was shocked at the overwhelming response from everyone, whom I'll list at the end of my book for you to check out, whether or not they got killed.

J.A. Barrios was the most excited. He actually corrected me on a few behavior ticks of his and ensured I was accurate. I remember the text message: *Dude, I wouldn't kick his boot and insult him. I'd spit right on his corpse.* Fair point, as I've seen Barrios spit on a car that nearly ran him down at a red light, like he was a camel eating Bubblicious Gum. Cailin also added her two cents. Switching *woman* to *bitch* was her idea and made the dialogue more natural. Brian rewrote some of his catch phrases to mirror dialogue he would say in real life—his most-favorite reply—saying *word*, when he's agreeing to a plan—and including references to his favorite childhood films that he also mentions in each of his own published novels, as a personal joke to his readers.

More natural. That was what I was shooting for here. I wanted some of the most-grounded people you'd meet. I love writing characters, especially if they actually exist! You should take my casts' actions with a grain of salt. We all say we'd be John Rambo but would quickly morph into a loaded diaper the second things hit the fan. I knew I would have fun with everyone.

Whether I killed off someone or they lived has nothing to do with my level of respect or love for them. The fact they're in my book means I absolutely love them as a person and as a creative. It was something I had been clear about when writing *FUBAR*. Just because I killed off Specialist So-and-So doesn't mean I hated them. It's often a decision I have to sit with for a bit and decide if it's their time in the book or not.

That's the best part, though—the killing off a character. They often suggested the death of their character! Either the method or the suggestion that "Well, let's be honest. I'd be dead." I took a lot of that into consideration. The intended effect was one of natural, unhurried authenticity. In contrast, others felt jarring, as though someone had been abruptly taken from you.

One author friend, Sawney Hatton, had a discussion with me at a convention where we joked about killing him off at the start of Chapter 1—a *Christmas Carol* type of send-off. "Sawney was dead from the start." The jokes became so silly that, at one point, he was killed off on the title page and opening copywrite stuff! "All rights reserved. Sawney Hatton was killed. Copyright 2025."

It was almost more fun to speculate about the story than it was to write, honestly. I just hope those of you reading this enjoy it as much as I enjoyed writing it. Maybe you'll keep your head on a swivel when you're at the next event, wondering if someone is watching you? I'll see you at the end of this entire nightmare!

PRE-CONVENTION

> *"You're braver than you believe,*
> *and stronger than you seem, and smarter*
> *than you think."*
>
> — A. A. Milne, Christopher
> Robin

NIGHTMARES UNBOUND IS LIVE! ARE YOU ALIVE?

You are cordially invited to attend the most spectacular convention in this region of the Appalachian Mountains. Horror! Anime! Science Fiction! Everything you can imagine. Get ready for a three-day event that will be a feast for the senses and leave everyone satisfied! We're showcasing numerous true crime authors, whose chilling tales will send shivers down your spine; a few die-hard horror enthusiasts, ready to share their terrifying discoveries; and renowned figures from the annals of pop culture, adding a touch of celebrity glamour to the event! Attendees can enjoy a variety of entertainment at the event, including thrilling sideshow acts with daring feats, spellbinding live readings, and a captivating magic show with illusions that defy explanation. Prepare to be amazed by the dazzling displays and the electrifying energy of this convention—sights and sounds that will leave you breathless. Suitable for people of all ages! Snag deeply discounted tickets this Black Friday; it's a limited offer you won't want to miss! Hurry! Get them now, before it's too late! You'll be dying to come to our event!

11:37

Posts   **About   Photos   Videos   More ▾**

the electrifying energy of this convention—sights and sounds that will leave you breathless. Suitable for people of all ages! Snag deeply discounted tickets this Black Friday; it's a limited-time offer you won't want to miss! Hurry! Get them now, before it's too late! You'll be dying to come to our event!

👍 7.9K   1.3K comments 817 shares

👍 Like   💬 Comment   📞 Send   ↪ Share

Home   Video   Friends   Marketplace   Notifications   Menu

Nightmares Unbound

CHAPTER 1

"The wise man does not expose himself needlessly to danger, since there are few things for which he cares sufficiently; but he is willing, in great crises, to give even his life—knowing that under certain conditions it is not worthwhile to live."

— *Aristotle*

I didn't know what to make of the email when I saw it. At first, I thought it was a scam—yet another baiting email appearing in my inbox, its insidious request for personal information detailing a clear path to my mother's maiden name and the street of my childhood home. Any quick search engine hit would answer any and all of those questions, for sure. Johnson and King Court, for anyone who'd be curious. Do with that what you will. Doubtful it would get you very far.

Something about the message struck me differently. I was invited by none other than horror convention runner Benjamin Parker and film director Alexander Mayfield! We've heard of these guys. By *we*, I clearly mean my author circle and me. It's such an exclusive event to get into. Sure, it had humble beginnings at a Holiday Inn conference room, sporting no more than fifteen vendors (so the website says), but it is unrecognizable as the literary behemoth it has become. Parker knew his shit, and teaming with Mayfield this year is a power move at best. I scoped out the website a bit more and clicked around on their social media posts.

Everything about it seemed legit, but I needed to be sure. You never know these days. I minored in cyber security and everything is suspicious to me these days. However, doing my homework, I found the email on the "Contact Us" page. I decided to fill out my concerns into the small white boxes and submitted them into the void of the Internet.

"And now... I wait," I muttered to nobody in particular.

My wife came into the room, preparing herself for work. She held a pair of heels in one hand and brushed her long brown hair with the other. She wore a pants suit, typical business fare for any high-paid executive but equally viable for a lowly shift manager at a consulting firm. My wife worked eight days a week, which worked out, as I practically lounged around in my SpongeBob pajamas for the same amount of time.

She braced herself against the off-blue painted wall of the office wall as she thrust her foot into one stubborn shoe.

"Is Violet awake yet?" she asked, trying to juggle forty tasks at once.

"Jesus, no. I forgot to wake her," I said, closing the laptop screen. "This one is on me. I see you're running late."

"Thanks. I mean it." She leaned in for a kiss as we passed by to our destinations.

I had no issue with taking our daughter to school. Often, I wasn't even awake at this hour. I happened to be plagued with the standard fare of nightmares that rattle around in my brain. I stared at my phone for an hour before deciding to be productive in my office. The world was silent at three in the morning, that was for sure.

With a quiet step, I moved toward Violet's room, the sound of soft music drifting from within. Light shuffling came from inside as I nudged the door open with a few gentle knocks.

"Come in!" a gentle voice greeted me from the other side.

As the door swung open, I glanced at the assortment of colors that adorned her walls. The lights were already on, illuminating the ornamented bedroom. She had posters of some K-Pop band I'd never heard of, plus some Disney Pop Princess, among other colorful characters. I insisted she have some Disney Princesses and maybe even a Wonder Woman poster to shake things up a bit. It was what could be expected from a typical girl's room, I'd assumed. Vastly different from my posters of Korn, *Evil Dead,* and *Doom.* To each their own, I suppose.

I watched my six-years-old daughter lace her own shoes. Poorly, may I add, but by God, she tried. She never did quite master the rabbit and the tree bit. She could go over, but once it went under, everything went to pot.

"Need some help, sweetie?" I asked, gesturing toward the shoes.

"Bye, Violet! Bye, Harry!" Audrey called from the living room.

"Bye, Mommy!" Violet belted out before the door slammed.

Audrey and I had been married for nearly fifteen years. She had been there for the ups and downs. Mostly the downs. I had struggled to get into writing fresh out of college, but she stuck with it. While I had pretended to be a wordsmith, she buckled down at a nine-to-five, keeping the bills paid. I had felt like such a piece of shit for years. After year eight, the tables turned, if only a gentle rotation. My first published work, *The Killer Strikes at Dawn,* had become an international hit! I topped the charts. I had struck gold on the first hit, as they say.

In the years to follow, several *New York Times* bestsellers had been squeezed out of my fingertips and onto the keyboard. I'd managed to write a handful of crime novels, and even took my try at a young adult dystopian story. The teeny bopper angst was enough to tell me that I wasn't cut out for that line of work. My stories needed to be visceral, meaty, and full of grown-up drama. Can't blame a guy for trying, though.

"Daddy, can we get McDonald's on the way to school?" Violet asked as I finished tying her shoes.

I checked my watch. "If you get moving right now, yes. Grab your lunch in the kitchen. Mommy packed it for you."

Even though Audrey worked her ass off while I sat around in last week's pajamas, she still insisted on making Violet's lunch. It's not that I was lazy, it was just that I had nowhere to be in particular. I would lounge around in my finest slum-wear without a care in the world. The life of an author, I suppose. Though I usually stuck to jeans and a tee-shirt, the occasional book signing would warrant a more respectable ensemble—a crisp dress shirt and smart trousers.

"I'm almost ready, Daddy!"

"Ok, Peanut!" I called back to Violet.

Glancing at my watch, I noted the time with a feeling of mild anxiety. Rain or shine, through thick and thin, my watch remained steadfastly on my wrist. It was a sleek, black smartwatch, with a comfortable band—a Christmas gift from my wife, three years ago. The device monitored my physical activity, recording my heart rate and the number of steps I took, with astonishing accuracy. I guess she had been worried about me and got me a micro-manager for my daily activities. I will admit, it was useful to hear a buzz to tell me that I'd been sitting on my ass for too long. The little animation of the guy standing up and stretching always cracked me up. Sure, I would get right up and start doing lunges because my watch said so.

Violet strutted out dressed in what I can only describe as a six-year-old's fever dream. She wore so many layers that I'd assumed I had been thrust back into the '80s, or even the '90s grunge era. Two mismatched socks adorned her feet, and her pants were high-rise capris, showcasing the artwork of SpongeBob and My Little Pony riding up each calf.

"Are you going to change? Mommy walks me into the school now," Violet said, grabbing her lunch from the countertop.

I glanced at my stained gray sweats—the University of Maryland Alumni emblazoned on the chest, pocked with stains of Cheetos and what I can assume, or hope, was mustard.

"Two shakes, sweetie," I said, jetting to the bedroom to quickly change.

Once I was in normal human clothing, I felt I was presentable enough to go out into the world. I grabbed the keys, jammed them into my jeans pocket, and shoved my wallet into my back pocket. My cellphone was charging in the kitchen, which I snagged before pushing Violet to the door.

Once on the highway, I asked her what her choice of fine dining would be this wonderful morning. We rode past everything from the local diner to the Golden Arches. She continued to pleat the ruffles on the poofy dress she insisted on wearing over the capri leggings.

"You gotta pick something, honey," I said defeatedly as we passed a Wendy's.

"That place!" Violet bounced in her seat! "That one!"

As I glanced up, my eyes were met with the sight of a Taco Bell, its colorful sign accentuated against the surrounding buildings. Their breakfast was awful; cold eggs and rubbery sausage nauseated me. I swore they had the fastest digestion rate of any food I'd ever eaten. I'd be lucky to make it to Vi's class before nearly having a blow-out.

"Taco Bell?" I confirmed with her.

Violet exchanged an enthusiastic head bobble as I pulled into the drive-thru. We ordered her breakfast taco and a small soda to go, and I opted out of anything, much to Violet's dismay.

"No taco?" Violet asked as she reached into the bag for hers.

"At my age? That taco would do more damage than a wrecking ball in a china shop, honey."

I was half right. Part of me wanted to grab one of those tortilla-wrapped diarrhea makers. The other half of me didn't want to be praying to the porcelain gods for the rest of the day. As I merged onto the main highway, my phone buzzed. It was Brian. It was too early to hear from him, honestly.

Brian was a fellow author. We'd done several book tours together, building a crazy relationship where we'd boast about the good ones and would rip apart the bad ones. We had spoken on panels together, and he had even brought his daughter to help celebrate Violet's most recent sixth birthday. Brian shared an adoration for the band REO Speedwagon with me. He loved to write the most macabre-filled mystery thrillers on the East Coast, in my opinion. He had even stopped working as a full-time security guard when his books had taken off, much like how I had given up on working in the service industry when things had gotten good.

I reached for the receiver button on my car. "Yo!"

"Hey, man. It's Brian."

"I got caller ID on the phone now, bud. Welcome to the future. What's up?"

"Oh, right. Hey, you driving? Is this a bad time?" Brian asked.

"No, I got Vi in the car right now, taking her to school. I got five minutes. What's up?"

"HI MISTER BRIAN!!!" Violet shrieked while holding back a face full of egg and tortilla.

I pulled around the corner to the back road that led to Violet's school, just as someone tried to skirt around me in their car and take the same turn. I violently honked and carefully chose my words.

"Jesus Christ, you okay?" Brian asked.

"No, some jackass almost killed Daddy!" Violet quickly answered.

"Vi!" I said, while laughing a bit. "Anyway, what's up, man?"

"I got this email today from some convention, Nightmares Unbound or whatever, and didn't know if you got in. Apparently they're requesting my presence."

I crept to a stop sign. "Same. I wasn't sure if it was legit or not myself."

"Ben Parker is an absolute legend of an event runner, dude!"

I paused for a moment. "Sounds like a superhero to me. Isn't that the name of someone?"

"I guess. Spider-Man? Uncle Ben?"

"I knew it! That was going to bother me all day," I said, pulling into Violet's school parking lot.

Brian chuckled a bit. "So, you doing it? My con buddy? Keep my sanity? I'll bring the amaretto!"

I shot a glance at Violet, who had her backpack in hand, clutching her lunch pail in her fist.

"Yeah, man. I'll email Ben to tell them I'm in if you're in. Sounds, I dunno, killer?"

"I see what you did there!" Brian jested. "Okay, I'll let you go. Update me with your details. I'll load in on Thursday. Maybe we can grab a beer and a burger?"

I shut off the engine and took a deep breath. "Yeah, sounds good, dude. I'll hit you up when I confirm and we'll figure it out."

"Word. Well, I'll let you get going. Good talking to you. Have a good day in school, Violet!" Brian said, then disconnected.

I looked at Violet. "You heard Mr. Brian. Be good!"

Violet grabbed the door handle. "He said to *have* a good day, not to *be* good."

She was right. She could always see through the lines with everything. I could absolutely see who she got her smart-ass-ness from. I got out and helped Violet from the car, and the two of us headed toward the school entrance. Mrs. Volkner waited by the main entrance, as always. She was a lovely, what I'd call *traditional,* schoolteacher, complete with the tight bun of hair and deep pockets to confiscate contraband from the students. I'd only assumed she had acquired larger pockets to compensate for the tablets and Nintendo's that found themselves being played under the school desk. I was glad things hadn't changed too drastically since I was in.

"And how are we today, Miss Violet?"

"I'm excited, Miss Volkner!" Violet cheered back, with a bit of a skip in her step.

I smiled and led my daughter toward her teacher. It was always hard to watch her grow up. Today was the day I would start work on my novel, so as much as I would have loved stand there and watch the now vacant doorway, I needed to get some progress done. Procrastination was my normal setting. I'd been waffling on three story ideas, and none of them gripped me. One was about a detective and a reporter who teamed up to nab a serial killer, but I lacked the real meat of the story in my mind. The other was about a guy who was haunted by the death of his childhood friend, but I didn't have an angle for it. The last involved a toaster. I guess this was what they called writer's block. I hated it.

CHAPTER 2

*"Normally in dangerous situations,
I have a getaway car."*

— *Sacha Baron Cohen*

Harry Carpenter

"**J**esus H. Christ!" I belted from my office as something from outside came crashing to the floor in a cacophony of sounds.

Adrenaline surged as I leaped from my chair. My hand instantly gripped the doorknob, the shattering of glass still echoing in my ears. I was ready to confront whoever had dared violate my home. I expected a masked bandit but instead found Violet and Audrey standing over a disaster in the living room. It didn't take me long to figure out what had been destroyed.

"I'm sorry, babe. The cat just went after a fly, and this was in his way." Audrey shot a look at the cat.

Pigley made zero effort to apologize. He just sat there smugly on the sofa, licking his asshole. Imagine being a cat and having zero ramifications for what you did, your owners justifying everything with, "Well, he's a cat." Oh, to be a cat in the world for just a day. Pigley saw me glaring at him, and he immediately removed himself from the sofa to take refuge in his enormous cat gymnasium he got last Christmas.

I kneeled in the mess. My shadowbox full of awards, pins, and medals from the military was strewn about. Glass mixed with ribbons and wood throughout. I shooed away my family as I rose to stand over the mess. I grabbed my Combat Action Badge and noticed that this disaster could have been far worse. The medals were intact, just no longer housed in a beautiful shadow box that my father had given me before he passed.

"You know what? It was about time I found somewhere else to put these medals," I said, carefully collecting them to not slice open my hand on the exposed glass edges.

Audrey kneeled to help me retrieve a few. "I enjoyed having it in the living room. It meant so much to you, and it was such a good talking point at parties."

I took a moment to glance at the dirt outline that surrounded where the shadowbox used to reside. My God did walls get dirty when you couldn't tell the difference. Violet jumped over the glass and toward her bedroom.

"Careful! You'll get hurt if you do that again," Audrey yelled to her.

"I have to finish working on my diorama for class! Miss Volkner gave us a fun project to complete!"

With that, Violet disappeared around the corner to her bedroom. She'd been working on a holiday shoebox diorama for the past few weeks, ever since Thanksgiving break. It was a top-secret project, and I was only privy to the shopping lists she had provided. Tin foil was a hot commodity around this house, as Vi would constantly steal it all from the drawer. I eventually had asked if she needed foil and grabbed her a large roll on my next outing to Wal-Mart.

I collected my awards, pins, and buttons in one hand and sauntered to my office. On my desk laid a very nice carved box from my grandmother, with my name engraved. I figured I'd remove some of the larger mementos, such as a replica fingerboard toy of the skateboard I used to own when I was much younger, as well as some other very hard, less sensitive and breakable items. I dumped a handful of medals into the box and resecured the lid to ensure their safekeeping until I figured out a new option.

To maintain a professional atmosphere, I barred Pigley from my office, anticipating his disruptive presence and the inevitable chaos that would follow. He might be twenty-three pounds, but my God could he move. I returned to the living room to assist, only to find Audrey had already cleaned the mess.

"I could have helped with that, you know," I said. "Isn't it enough that you work a hundred hours a week?"

"Yeah, but I know you're trying to figure out your new book plot. You know what they say about breaking the writer's mojo when he's on a roll!"

I smiled. For years, Audrey had sworn this was a dumb hobby and was a waste of my time. I was an amateur writer and not a big and famous one, like Stephen King. Hell, even King had to pay his dues with some bad books and short stories once in a while. Once my first hit book, *The Killer Strikes at Dawn*, made its way up the charts, eventually becoming a bestseller on not only *New York Times* but also on Amazon, I allowed myself a bit of smugness.

I wrote some duds before that one really hit, though. *Killer Strikes* was my magnum opus. It was my Mona Lisa, as far as I was concerned. Unlike Michelangelo, I couldn't muster a follow-up hit in over a year. For a Ninja Turtle, that guy could sure paint. That joke is in there for Violet, because it goes over *sooo well* at parties when her friends are around. Ninja Turtles aren't cool anymore, I guess. Tell that to the umpteenth reboot of the franchise though.

"Hey, Audrey, got a sec?" I asked, placing the broom in the closet designed specifically for them.

Audrey paused and met my gaze.

"There's this big event I was invited to as a special guest. I haven't done much of these recently, outside of libraries and a few small bookstores in the area."

"Okay...?"

"Well, it's for the entire weekend. I'm used to the one-day adventures. This is about an hour from the house, which is nice, but I'll likely stay overnight to save on tolls, gas, and my road rage in the traffic."

Audrey smiled. "Well, it sounds like you have finally made it, bigshot. I'm proud of you!"

She threw her arms around my neck as I continued my story.

"It's some big horror convention. Brian insists I join him so he's not fully miserable."

Audrey backed up a bit, arms still around my neck. "Are you boys going to have an adult with you?"

I smiled. "So, you're cool with it?"

Audrey moved toward the kitchen and grabbed a water bottle from the fridge. "Yeah, I'm as good as can be. I'd hate for you to be away for so long. Is it soon?"

"Thankfully not until well after the holidays. It's in February. Chances are, it'll get snowed out, and they'll cancel or postpone, and I won't have to go anywhere."

Audrey furrowed her eyebrow. "Do you *not* want to go?"

"It's not that I don't want to go. I always have fun with these things," I said, collecting any remaining pieces of glass from the floor before Audrey passed me the broom. "It's just the buildup. The prep. Making sure I have stock of my books, signage, and the energy to be at an event for ten to twelve hours a day."

Audrey nodded in agreement as she sipped her water. Pigley trodded along the living room floor as if he hadn't just committed the murder of a shadowbox. I finished cleaning the rest of the glass, gave it a once over with the Dust Buster, and went to check on Violet's progress of her project.

CHAPTER 3

"It must have courage, cunning, and, above all, it must be able to reason."

— Richard Connel, General Zaroff, The Most Dangerous Game

*T*hanksgiving came and went, as did Christmas. We celebrated with the banging of pots and pans for the new year and drank faux champagne with Violet around 9 p.m., which we insisted was the start of the new year. This was going to be the year. I would get out of the writing funk and actually pen something. By pen, I mean sit on my laptop and do something other than scroll mindlessly through Facebook or play solitaire. The menacing blinking line mocked me with each fade in, returning to remind me of the nothingness that followed.

Presently I had completed a dedication page and the Other Works page. Progress. I was almost done, right? I'd take myself out to a local eatery, a crepe shop tucked away in a shopping center. The owners never cared that I took up a table to write. I would pay for my food and would purchase at least two Cokes during my stay. The trouble with this place was with one of the owners, Paul. He was always a distraction, asking me the latest thoughts on wrestling or about a newly released horror movie. I'd stare at my screen for a moment, then be sidelined for an hour discussing whether Mankind was the best portrayal Mick Foley could do, or if it was Cactus Jack.

Today was no different. I sat down and enjoyed the crepe that bore my namesake. It was something the owners liked to do. If someone of notoriety lived in the community *and* were a patron of their restaurant, they'd name a dish after them. Mine included an absurd amount of bacon, which I assumed would be the death of me. Sitting in this quaint little restaurant, I watched through the large glass windows of the front of the store as dozens of families skated on the ice rink across the way in the park.

"How about that match last night?" Paul asked, as he sat on a milk crate next to the counter.

I had been here for fifteen minutes. I had already eaten and planned to take the rest of the time to write some of this new novel—or, at least, pretend to. The derailment was earlier than usual, since the crowd hadn't swept through the restaurant yet.

"I didn't watch," I replied.

"You missed a hell of a match, man. Look, I know it's all staged or acted out or whatever, but goooooddaaaaamn that was a way to end a show!"

I had watched a few highlights on a Facebook reel or two but hadn't actually watched the show. Pausing for a moment, I vividly remembered it—the creak of the ladder, the tension in the air before the triple super plex, then the collective gasp of the audience. It was rough to watch, and while I agreed wrestling was scripted—or *fake*, as the general public would say—I couldn't deny the physicality.

"I saw the ladder bit."

"Dude. Can you imagine being the little guy at the top? That's gotta be terrifying! They're, what? Like three stories up at that point?"

I studied Paul for a moment. This was when the derailment took place. I instantly Googled how high the wrestlers were during the penultimate move. "Four-point-two stories high, bud."

"Jaysus. Can you imagine, though?"

Almost as a saving grace, a crowd of bundled-up up children, with their equally frozen parents, rushed the counter from the skate rink, demanding hot chocolates, teas, and coffee, allowing me to refocus on the story. I had a few ideas bouncing around but couldn't quite get to where I needed to be with the narrative. The idea was a zombie apocalypse, but every time I went down the road with it, it turned into more TV cliché bullshit that seemed to be everywhere these days. A part of me thought, *Why not just call the main guy* Rick *and get it over with?*

I putzed around for a bit on the computer before checking my email one last time. An email had arrived from the convention, from Benjamin Parker himself (or that of a mailer on his behalf.)

WONDERFUL VENDORS AND ESTEEMED GUESTS:

IT IS MY PLEASURE TO JOIN YOU IN THE EXCITEMENT THAT THIS YEAR'S NIGHTMARES UNBOUND WILL BE BIGGER THAN EVER! EVER SINCE ITS CONCEPTION, I'VE WANTED TO FOCUS ON ONE THING: TO BRING EVERYONE AN OUTSTANDING EVENT AND LAY IT ALL ON THE LINE! THIS YEAR, OUR SPONSORSHIP WITH ALEXANDER MAYFIELD WILL ENABLE US TO GO BIGGER, BADDER, AND BLOODIER THAN EVER BEFORE!

THIS YEAR, WE'RE FEATURING A QUALITY ILLUSIONIST ALL THE WAY FROM CALIFORNIA, WHO HAS EVEN STUMPED THE LIKES OF PENN & TELLER! THERE'S A FREAKSHOW SIDESHOW ACT, AND SEVERAL FILM SCREENINGS TAKING PLACE UNDER OUR ROOF! WE'RE DELIGHTED TO WELCOME YOU TO THE EVENT!

BELOW ARE THE DETAILS FOR LOADING IN, AS WELL AS WHERE TO CHECK IN AND THINGS TO EXPECT! WE'RE ALSO INCLUDING THE LINKS TO SEVERAL HOTELS IN

THE AREA, SHOULD YOU STILL NOT HAVE ONE BOOKED! THANKS AGAIN, AND WE'LL SEE YOU IN A FEW WEEKS!

The email continued about where and when to set up, policies and procedures for getting inside, and what we can do. It was hard to believe that time had moved fast enough that the convention was just a short three weeks away. I felt like it had just been September! How did time move this fast? I really wished I had a new book to debut for this event. As I finished updating my phone calendar with the load-in times, it buzzed in my hand.

"Yo!" I said to Brian as I picked up the phone.

"What's up, man? Anyway, you got the email, didn't you?"

"Yes, I just got it. I'm staying at a Hampton Inn a few blocks away. Did you snag a room?"

"'ll actually just drive it each day. Save myself a few hundred bucks," Brian said assertively.

"I hear that. I can't deal with the traffic. The highway just pisses me off, and if I was pulling into this place at eight a.m. each day, I can't see me leaving the house so early in the morning."

"That's fair. Well, I wanted to know if you'd like to grab brunch with us on Friday before we have to set up at the event. I figure we drop our books, set the tables, and grab some grub."

"Who's the 'us' you're talking about?"

Brian paused. "Hold on. I'm just checking the group text to see who's in."

I held for a moment. The children were filing out to the skate rink again, hot chocolates in hand.

"Oh, here we go. It's me. I assume you, right? We're looking at the usual suspects: Callie, Marissa, Jenny, and Dan. I'm waiting to hear from Barrios and a few others," Brian rattled off.

"Ooh. A nice reunion of sorts? This should be good."

I hadn't seen some of these faces since I debuted my last novel more than a year ago. I contained my excitement, but I loved seeing these folks. My hiatus of book tours was starting to weigh on me, as I became more and more of a homebody.

"I'm pretty pumped, man. Looking forward to it. Anyway, we'll game plan somewhere to eat, but if you have any suggestions in the area, I'm open for ideas," Brian said. "I'll touch base with you before the event. Cool?"

"Works for me. Catch you later."

Before I finished saying *later*, Brian had already disconnected. I was excited to see a lot of the familiar faces I typically would find at the East Coast horror events. A year and a half had passed since I'd last seen Barrios, and the reunion was exciting. I was glad to see we were getting the band back together, as they say.

Before Paul could come to me with more wrestling talk, I had shut down my laptop and packed up.

"Hey, man. Good seeing you, as always. Tell the wifey I said hi."

I extended a fist bump to him. "Same to you. Hope your wife and the kiddo are doing good. Tell your mom I said hi," I said as I connected for the fist bump and sauntered toward the door.

I checked my watch and saw it was nearly 3 p.m. I needed to pick up Violet and get home to start dinner. I quickly sped toward her school, trying my best to avoid the red lights where I could. She would get dismissed in a few moments, and I didn't have any time to spare.

CHAPTER 4

*"Death is but a door. Time is but a
window. I'll be back."*

— *Vigo the Carpathian,*
Ghostbusters II

I sat for what felt like ages in the parking lot. All the children were either ushered onto a yellow bus or the parents had picked them up already. A frequent observation was how many parents did the pickup in their pajamas. I barely had what could pass as a job, but at least I put on jeans and a tee-shirt today. I'd never understand that. It wasn't the 1930s, where we had to get in a three-piece suit to see a film, but still. Maybe that was just me. As I thought about where our standards as a society were, I scanned the lot at the sparse selection of children still lingering about. Not one of them was my kid. I killed the engine and made my way inside.

The school hallways were unfamiliar to me. When I grew up, we had red lockers, and we could customize, be creative, or decorate them. Paper cutouts, drawings, and scrabbled musings of me and my fellow classmates had adorned the walls. The seasonal theme in November meant an overwhelming yet delightful display of hand turkeys—a colorful, slightly chaotic, and wonderfully festive sight. These walls were—how do I put this—cold. This place had no substance. Everything felt very administrative and businesslike, like the posters about seeing something and saying something or how to deal with an active threat. It was a lot.

When I went to school, we had Got Milk posters of Michael Jordan towering over us. Scruff McGruff warned us to take a bite out of crime, at best. I rounded the corner to the administrator's office as an active shooter drill poster greeted me. Tips to take if you find yourself in danger. What a world we lived in, right? Normally I'd have shrugged this off, but it was an all-to-real situation that my kid could find herself in and was a bit close to home. I'd actively decided to join a profession for a half decade where I was aware folks would be shooting at me. I'd never dream of doing it in grade school.

As the administrative office came into view, I recognized a familiar hairstyle hovering just above the glass window. My kid was in the office. Like father, like daughter. I spent half my education sitting in these offices. I had never really been problematic, but they had assumed I was. Things had gotten crazy in the '90s, when those two ding-dongs decided to shoot up their high school. While they hadn't been the first, they were absolutely the biggest names of our generation, opening the flood gates for a world that we find ourselves in now. Teachers had constantly dragged me into the office for wearing dark clothing, listening to so-called scary rock and roll, and having black fingernails from time to time. I knew why I had been in the office, but why was Violet?

"Are you Violet's father?" the administrative assistant asked from behind her desk.

"Depends. What did she do?" I joked. She was unamused.

"Violet seems to have found herself in a bit of a scuffle in the lunchroom just before dismissal. She was found fighting one of her classmates."

I faced Violet. She was sitting in a rather aggressive stance, with her arms crossed, sporting the largest frown. I had to activate dad-mode. "Vi, what happened? What girl were you fighting?"

"*Boy.* She was fighting a boy," the assistant corrected.

I raised an eyebrow that would have made The Rock proud. "A *boy?*"

"He started it!" Violet threw her arms down at her sides as she stood.

I looked at the administrator for clarification, because I figured I would get nothing but resistance from Violet going forward.

"There were some children waiting for dismissal in the lunchroom when the scuffle took place. By the time Mr. Logue and Mrs. Dombrowski could break it up, she had already pummeled three boys."

Internally, I wanted to high-five my child. Had she kicked the shit out of three boys? Please tell me that they were in a grade higher and twice her size. On the other hand, externally, I had to play professional dad. "These boys, what was the reasoning behind this whole thing? Were they in the same class?"

The administrative assistant stood and signaled to someone just out of view. A large Black male wearing a cardigan sweater and a tiny blonde woman in the cliché deep-pocketed one-piece dress entered the room.

"Mr. Carpenter, I presume?" the man asked.

I wanted to fire off with my usual, "Depends, are you the cops?" but this was neither the time nor the place. "I am. And you are?"

"I'm Mister Logue, and this here is Mrs. Dombrowski. We were the teachers assigned to man the fort, so to speak, in the cafeteria when the altercation broke out."

I proffered my hand to shake both of theirs.

"I'm sorry this happened, honestly. Are the other students okay?" I asked, feigning concern.

Dombrowski took the reins for this question. "They are doing okay. The nurse just finished patching them up about ten minutes ago."

Patching them up? Good gravy, Vi, what did you do?

"It's shocking that she could do this to a boy twice her size and two years her senior," Logue added. "It took all my strength to break through the chaos, and I was a Marine!"

"Oh? I was Army myself. When and where?" I asked, trying to change the subject. Logue went for the bait immediately.

"I was in around oh-five to ten. I wanted to jump in and hit the ground right after 9/11, but my grandmother wouldn't let me. Once I hit twenty, I took my chance."

I nodded and eyed Dombrowski. "Oh, no. I recently graduated college and only started teaching here two years ago. I'm not cut out to be a Marine."

The administrative assistant cleared her throat, as if to get everyone back on track. "What are we to do about this?"

I observed Violet, who rapidly swung her feet in the chair that seemed far too large for her—almost comically large, like a scene from *Alice in Wonderland.*

"Jimmy started it! He said I didn't have rizz and was cheugy!"

I stared blankly for what felt like an eternity. The gears were turning, but nothing was processing. What the absolute hell was my daughter saying? This may as well be a foreign language.

"Rizz, or cheugy, are some insults the kids have been picking up from TikTok or YouTube lately, for clarification," Logue said. "Cheugy is a new way to say lame, wack, or uncool."

"Then just say lame," I exclaimed, rubbing the bridge of my nose as I tried to process.

The administrative assistant reined it in once more. "It is my recommendation that young Violet get involved with a hobby or a sport to use as an outlet. She has anger that needs to be handled in a manner that is safe, therapeutic, and controllable."

I stared at Violet. "She's harmless! It sounds like they picked on her first, if I'm being honest."

"Be that as it may, we cannot condone her physical retaliation. We stress that if there is an issue, please alert a member of the faculty, and we will deal with it."

"So, you want Violet to be a narc? Won't that just cause even more bullying?"

Mr. Logue chuckled; I was glad I wasn't the only sane one in the room.

"Mister Carpenter, if Violet doesn't get her temper under control, we will be forced to take additional steps. We are hoping you can mediate and mitigate this before we are forced to act further."

I nodded. "I'll let her mother know, and we'll have a talk. Thank you for letting me know."

I grabbed Violet's hand and escorted her through the winding maze of anti-bullying, active-shooter, and other posters.

Once I saw sunlight, I knew we were home free. I hated being inside schools, and I had a sneaking suspicion that Violet would grow to share my sentiments.

"So, you really nailed that boy?" I asked, pushing the door open to the parking lot.

"Jimmy knows what he did. He's always picking on me. He kicked me last week. This week he threw his bottle of water at me. And today he said those things about me! And he's mean, and he's smelly and a jerk and—"

"I get it. Don't worry about it. I'll talk to your mother, but she doesn't need to know everything. I got picked on at school too. The last thing I want you to do is run to a teacher every time something happens."

"I know, Daddy. Snitches get stitches!" Violet chimed in.

I raised my kid well. With an audible creak, I opened the back door, and Violet scrambled inside to buckle herself. I tossed her bookbag into the front seat and closed that before inspecting Violet was locked and loaded, ready to roll out.

"Can I have a moment?" a booming voice came from behind me.

I jolted in place before whirring around to see.

"Oh, Mister Logue! Semper Fi and all that."

"I just wanted to talk to you offline and off record, if that's okay?"

I looked at Violet, who was watching me through the window. It was a bit chilly, but I could give him a moment of my time, I supposed. "Shoot."

"If we're being honest, Jimmy had that coming. That kid is such a pain in my ass, and if I was forty years younger, I'd have likely taken him out to the playground to rearrange his face. Problem is, we're living in today's world."

"I hear that," I interjected.

"Bottom line," Logue said, as he knife-handed while talking, "she'll want to stick up for herself, but please talk to her about times and places. Not trying to condone violence, I'm just stressing the fact that she needs restraint and control. I'm hoping you understand where I'm coming from."

I nodded. "If anyone gets it, I do. I was bullied as a kid, and whenever I fought back, I got in trouble, too. I'm tracking what you're saying."

"You think it was any easier being one of three Black kids in my school back in the day? I completely understand it. Bullies are bullies; they just adapt to the times. If there's one thing they're good at, it's gaming the system. Please encourage Violet to be smarter in her actions, hear?"

I smiled a bit. This Logue fellow was a straight shooter. Nothing I loved more than to meet someone who didn't just blow smoke up my ass and tell me what I wanted to hear or adhered to a set of rules, as if they were gospel. I could tell he was a wonderful teacher and *got* it.

"Thank you for taking a few moments to speak with me; I appreciate your time," I reached to shake his hand, which he received. "Thanks, Mr. Logue."

"Please, it's *Allen,*" he said, then headed down the path toward the school.

I hopped in the car and started the engine.

"Do we have to tell Mommy?" Violet asked.

I adjusted the radio volume. "We have to tell her something. They'll probably mail a letter home, and we need to prepare for that."

The fact I was conspiring with my child was a testament to my character. I also knew what it was like to be in trouble for something that wasn't my fault when nobody had my back. It was a hellacious way to trudge through life. I wanted Violet to know I'd do anything for her. Hell, I'd take a bullet for her. And seeing how many posters hung around that school, I had a pretty high chance of getting hit by a stray while picking her up one day.

"I'm sorry I did that," Violet said.

The level of remorse was high in her voice. I don't think she was genuinely sorry she beat the absolute taste out of that boy's mouth, but I think she's sorry it got to the point that it did. She's a good kid, just very defensive.

I turned the ignition key to begin our long drive home. "I get that, Vi. Really, I do. I'm not sorry you retaliated. It's just that I wish we could keep you from being picked on and that this kid would just leave you alone. What's his beef, anyhow?"

"His what?" Violet giggled slightly.

"His beef. You know, his problem with you," I tried to clarify. "Wait, you know this *rizz* or whatever but not *beef*?"

"He's just a big meanie. I don't know.I don't want to talk about him anymore. Can I just go to my room when we get home?"

I understood that message. I turned the radio knob to increase the volume and took the least chatty ride home as we jammed out to the soundtrack to *Descendants*. Sacrifices were made to bring up her spirits, clearly. It would be a long drive home.

CHAPTER 5

"Here all suspicion must be abandoned, All cowardice must be extinct."

— Dante Alighieri, Inferno

"What do you mean, she had a fight?" Audrey tossed her jacket and purse onto the sofa.

I figured she'd find out either way, so it was best to ease it in before she got a letter in the mail or received a phone call. "She's fine. Some bully at school kept picking on her, so she stood up to them. Case closed."

"Case closed? Is the other girl okay? What are her parents saying?"

"*His*, and he's two years older and twice her size."

Audrey gave pause to my statement before shifting gears entirely. She paced around the living room for a moment before the gears had finally clicked into position for her. "And this is two weeks before you go away?"

"I'm only gone the weekend. It'll be fine."

Audrey sat on the edge of the ottoman to contemplate for a moment. She was focused, but also had an expression of, *It's too late in the day after work to be dealing with this madness.*

"She's fine. The boy is mostly fine. Administration is upset but let them be. Mr. Logue seems to be more or less on the same page as us, so she has some sort of ally in this matter on the inside."

Audrey stood, smoothing out her work shirt. She took several deep breaths before heading into Violet's room.

I stood silent, only for a moment, before heading in behind.

"Violet, what happened at school today?" Audrey asked.

Violet stopped coloring at her desk and looked up. "Jimmy was being mean."

Audrey's expression changed. "Jimmy? Again?" She faced me. "Jimmy? You couldn't have told me it was Jimmy?"

I had honestly forgotten the boy's name. I assumed he was the bully flavor of the week, and it wouldn't matter, but, as usual, I was dead wrong. "Yes?"

"Jimmy has been picking on her for weeks now! He came by the house last week to drop off a bag of shi—poop. He left a bag of poop, gift wrapped for Violet to find. And she did."

"And where was I?" I asked harmlessly.

"Out. Probably writing or pretending to write at a Burger King or something like you always do."

I was eating crepes, but now we're just pulling hairs at this point.

"I'm sorry. Why didn't anyone tell me?"

"Because she was probably too embarrassed to say someone sent her a box of doo-doo. It fell on me to handle it, and I and lost sight of it by the time we got to dinner that night."

I sat and chewed on that statement. I was insulted, had found out my daughter had been assaulted, and that my wife had to deal with a bag of shit on the porch in my absence. It wasn't like I pretended to be writing, but I found myself easily distracted by videogames and other more interesting things.

"Well, it's handled now. I got involved and they're dismissing it. Because Violet is much smaller and this kid is notoriously a hellion, they're not going further with a suspension or anything on her record," I added.

Audrey pursed her lips and sighed. "Next time, call me?"

"What? When your cellphone isn't on, and God forbid I call, and you have to put me on hold? The school *did* try to call you."

I realized my tone was getting hostile, and I was getting more sarcastic and snarkier the more I talked. I walked toward the kitchen to spare Vi of any more of this. Audrey didn't follow. Seeing her strained expression as she dealt with Violet, I wisely chose to drop the subject. To avoid my responsibilities, I returned to my laptop to obsessively check emails, book sales, and Facebook— anything to distract me from what was happening in my own home.

Another email had come through, this time from Alexander Mayfield himself. It was a little odd, because the convention had already sent me details on when and where to set up. I skimmed through it. The email from Mayfield, seemingly a mass CCd personal email, looked innocuous enough.

Dearest Guest,

It is I, Alexander Mayfield. You may know my works such as Hostility on Floor 9, Corroded Crypt, *or even my recent blockbuster hit,* Office Offerings. *I am delighted to be working with Mister*

Parker on this event, and I look forward to working with each and every one of you personally. It thrills me to know how much creativity exists out there, knowing that you are some of the best and brightest minds in the thriller, horror, and splatterpunk industries.

If there is anything I can do to assist furthering your careers, such as offering a testimonial, a soundbite, or my support in any way, please do not hesitate to find me over the weekend.

Yours, bound in blood,

A.M.

What an email to read. I was interested in this event before, but this guy added to the joy. What a pompous buffoon. I took this as a "look at me and how good I am" post. The moment I finished reading the email, someone wasted no time in hitting Reply All.

Hello, Jason Alvarez, here. I just wanted to thank you for the support of my work, and I look forward to working with you over the weekend. I trust we will all have a splendiferous time, and it will truly be a haunting event to remember.

-Jason Alvarez, horror and thriller author, professional ghost hunter and paranormal expert.

There's always one, right?

Save for Jason's Reply-All email, which was never warranted, this was shaping up to be a pretty interesting event. I figured part of me should do my homework and see if any of Mayfield's films were streaming. They were guttural, visceral, and usually not my jam. I was a huge fan of the first *Saw*, but couldn't sit through the rest, or even *Hostel*. Mayfield's *Murder on the Upper Floor* was a bit out of my wheelhouse, as was *Sweat Lodge Slaughter*, including parts two and three of that series.

Something about his films didn't sit well with me. I'd never been a fan of the murder-porn genre. I loved a good supernatural thriller, Japanese horror, or even the classic slashers. They all had character. Mayfield's films? These were just gory for the sake of gore. These actors were truly captivating, their animalistic intensity and raw emotionality giving the impression that they weren't just acting but actually living and breathing their roles. Before being taken down from social media, I remembered one of the clips making its rounds on several platforms, becoming quite popular before its removal. Some chick cried for almost six minutes into the camera. She was covered in blood, apologizing and praying. Everything one could think of in the situation she found herself in.

The clip was from *Office Highrise Massacre 6*. A half-dozen lunatics took over some Dunder Mifflin-looking office and held all the employees captive, having them fight each other for survival. The final girl and some janitor were the last two, and they refused to kill each other. The clip that circulated was from the scene where the armed lunatics beat the janitor to death, and she took off in the confusion, locking herself in the ladies' room for a few moments of sweet solace.

Like I said, I didn't watch these films, but I did my homework. To put it frankly, these films were absolutely fucked. Mayfield had won a handful of awards for best direction, best script, among a plethora of other accolades. I don't know, call me old-fashioned, but there was something left to be desired with these types of films—especially those that had no purpose or heart to them. Why did I care? Why was I invested in these characters? There had been no plot development, and frankly, the found-footage genre should have died ages ago with *Blair Witch Project* or *Paranormal Activity*. Yet here we were, right?

With a quick tap of my thumb, I texted Brian, needing to ensure the detailed emails had reached him. This event was approaching soon, so I figured we should coordinate food plans, which was the only reason I absolutely loved attending events: the fine dining in new locations. Except for the time I had gotten food poisoning from a bad batch of chicken cordon bleu. To put it bluntly, I bleu out of my backend for the entire evening and had found myself fighting for the energy to sign books in the morning. Aside from that, however, I absolutely enjoyed trying to find a new joint to eat, and a sucker for chicken cordon bleu.

My phone rang almost immediately after sending my text.

"What's up? I'm driving right now," Brian said, with an ambient amount of road white noise to back up his statement.

I scrolled to the top of the email and opened a copy of the tab to navigate to the load-in details. "You got the emails? We gotta be in there early as balls on Friday to set up if we want to survive the city."

Brian swore at some idiot driver before replying. "Yeah, I didn't see the new one. Important or just a waste of time?"

"It was the director, Mayfield, expressing his gratitude for you being there."

"You're damn right he should be glad I'm there. Doesn't he know who I am?" Brian joked.

"I barely know who I am, let alone who you are," I jabbed back.

There was a brief pause, which I assume attributed to Brian needing to focus for a moment.

"Okay, good," Brian said. "I just didn't want to miss something worthwhile, you know?"

I thought for a second. "Oh, speaking of worthwhile, did you know Violet beat the shit out of some kid in school?"

"Shut the hell up! No! What? Tell me. Details, my friend," Brian pleaded, as if a high school girl getting the latest gossip in the girls' bathroom.

"Nothing much to share. Some boy, who got held back once or twice, got absolutely wrecked by her."

"You can't see it, but I'm high-fiving her through the phone."

The last thing I needed was Brian encouraging Violet. First, it was the kid in school, next she became some Batman-esque villain-hunting vigilante, trained under her mentor, Brian the, well, *would he be her butler?* That might make a good story for the future—Violent Violet, the Vigilante.

"Please don't push her anymore that she has been. It's bad enough you give her those self-defense lessons when you guys babysit her," I scolded.

"Okay, okay. How is she doing? For real this time?"

"She's fine. Just moving through it. Audrey was a bit rattled by it, because it's unlike Violet to be in trouble and get nearly suspended."

"Oh, they didn't throw the book at her?"

"No, surprisingly. I guess they couldn't do it this time because it's the first incident, and he really is twice her size. He's just about your size, though. Maybe you should fight him?"

"Ha-ha-ha. You're just a comedian, aren't you? Anyway, I'm pulling up to the house and I need to get myself situated. I have some things to do before I drive four hours to that event next week," Brian said.

"I get that. Well, talk to you maybe next Thursday or Friday?"

"Sounds good. Take care, man."

Brian disconnected the phone with that. I just stared at the emails, then decided I needed to pop one of Mayfield's movies on after everyone went to bed. Maybe I'll pick one of the *Office Massacre* films?

CHAPTER 6

""Just remember what ol' Jack Burton does when the earth quakes, and the poison arrows fall from the sky, and the pillars of Heaven shake. Yeah, Jack Burton just looks that big ol' storm right square in the eye and he says, 'Give me your best shot, pal. I can take it.'"

— *Jack Burton*, Big Trouble in Little China

The packing process is always hell. Between trying to remember to include all my books, marketing materials, and signage, I also needed to not neglect my personal effects. I didn't want to relive the incident in Philly back in 2015, where I had forgotten socks and underwear. The line at Wal-Mart was absolutely insane for zero reason, and I spent the better part of the night in a checkout line, holding a pair of briefs. I double checked my suitcase to ensure I didn't make a mistake. *Three for the weekend, and one in case I poop my pants.* The chances of me doing that were slim to none but never actually zero. Be prepared, as the great lion Scar once said, right? I was sure that was what he was singing about.

My usual assortment of button-up Hawaiian shirts took up one corner of the suitcase, while kooky horror and novelty tee-shirts filled the other half. I triple checked I had everything. All present and accounted for, it seemed. I tossed in the remaining essentials, including deodorant and my heartburn pills. I know I muttered something along the lines of a "Getting old sucks" mantra as I zipped my suitcase. My laptop and other electronics were housed in my laptop bag. It was zero hour. Time to load the car.

By the time I had tossed my sweater onto the front seat, my back was screaming. I shouldn't be loading in so much crap, but here we were. We always wanted to be grown-ups, right? The joy of eating an entire cake for dinner and nobody could tell us otherwise—except our digestive system had a lot to say, as it turned out. Oh, to be young again. Or, at the least, in shape. To go back even ten years ago, that was the dream.

I did my mental checks, physical checks, and over obsessed with the fact I had everything. I'd been burned too many times, finding out I was missing a banner, a sign, or even an entire book title. How could I sell parts two and three of a series when I was missing the first one? Well, that had killed three whole books for a weekend, that was how. I was clear about having all my goodies packed. Last thing on the list was a cooler full of my Coke and snacks. I could live off soda for an entire event. While everyone else tried the concession stand hotdogs, I'd be avoiding the intestinal discomfort by living off soda until the evening.

My phone buzzed as I slammed the trunk for the last time—Audrey calling from work.

"Hello?" I asked, just in case it was a coworker calling for something that may have happened at work.

"Hey, did you leave yet?" Audrey asked.

"No, I was actually just obsessively triple checking every single thing when you called."

I took a few laps around my car to check that the tires were still all on and that none were flat. Yes, it was odd, but I couldn't be the only one.

"Did you remember your large banner this time?" Audrey asked.

"Yes, and I have the smaller one, too. And the banner stand, before you ask."

"Remembered all your books?"

I smiled. "Yes, I have all of them. Even the poems." I paused momentarily. "Violet got sent to the office again today."

"What happened now?"

"More of the same, I guess? I tried to talk to the administration on my lunch break, but I ran out of time. I'm leaving work early today to snag her. Wish me luck, while I figure out what to do with this kid."

"She's just acting out from something. I'll talk to her when I get home on Sunday if this doesn't shake itself out by then."

"You better hope she's gotten it out of her system. I'll text you later while you're setting up and let you know what happened." A lot of noise came over the headset. "I have to go. Love you and talk to you later!"

After she hung up, I stared at my car, surveyed my yard for a moment, then shouted a slew of obscenities into the void. Perks of parenthood, I suppose. One day, your kid may grow up to be you. With a deep sigh, I took one last lap around the house before embarking on the long trek to the convention center. I had about an hour and a half ahead of me. Maybe an hour, based on the way I drive.

Pigley greeted me at the door as I entered the house. He rubbed on my legs, and I kneeled to scratch his head.

"Okay, fat boy. You be good this weekend. Don't eat anyone, or the furniture," I said, scratching behind his ear.

Pigley scrutinized me, as if offended—could cats get offended—then trotted toward his food bowl. I figured I should top him off. Depending on what might happen with Audrey and Vi tonight, they may get home late. He would act as if he was wasting away, just skin and bones, if no one fed him by dinnertime. As the dry food splashed into the bowl, Pigley grunted and waddled toward the bowl, reaffirming why we called him *Pigley.*

As a kitten, he would grunt—he hadn't even been fat then—and basically oink like a pig whenever he moved fast. We called him *Pigley* soon after, and it couldn't be a more fitting name.

I ran his tail between my index and middle finger as I stood to scan the house once more for some odd thing I may have forgotten. Everything was accounted for. One final pee before hitting the road, and I was off.

I hit the road, mentally checking I had everything. I pulled into the Royal Farms parking lot—my farthest landmark from the house to signify I would still have enough time to panic-return to the house for something I had forgotten, be it the credit card reader, an entire book to sell, or even a change of pants. I checked the back seat for my items once more and went inside to grab a soda for the road. It wasn't a long trip, but it always helped to have a Coke for the road.

I waited in line for self-checkout and played on my phone. Posts from fellow authors and artists, showcasing their tables' locations at Nightmares Unbound, filled my social media feed. I had failed to make a similar post, because I was never that good at social media. By the time it was my turn, I quickly scanned, paid, and returned to the car, barely looking up from my phone. Brian had posted something about his attendance and had included an image of the floor plan, highlighting his space. Once I sat in the car, I launched my phone's photo editor to do the same, making my first viable social media post in ages. Not since my last book had I showcased anything worthwhile, and that had been over a year or two ago. Several thumbs ups and heart emojis instantly greeted me. Mission accomplished, I had showcased signs of life!

THURSDAY

*"The mind plays tricks on you.
You play tricks back! It's like you're
unraveling a big cable-knit sweater that
someone keeps knitting and knitting and
knitting and knitting and knitting and
knitting and knitting..."*

— *Pee-Wee Herman,* Pee-Wee's
Big Adventure

CHAPTER 7

"Focus on your actions, not the outcome, it is all you can kontrol"

— *Liu Kang,* Mortal Kombat 1

Harry Carpenter

*T*he trip wasn't arduous at all. I hit a few spurts of slowed traffic, but nothing was a standstill. *Conan O'Brien Needs a Friend* kept my mind occupied for the trip. By two o'clock, Sona and Matt had fired back at Conan enough to make me laugh as the most asinine drivers played leapfrog around me. By four, I had pulled up to the Hampton Inn very near to the event center Nightmares Unbound was taking place. Surprisingly, for a big event happening, there wasn't too much signage in the area. I shut off the car and texted Brian to let him know I was in town. He didn't reply right away, so I could only assume he was driving or was in the middle of something. The neighborhood was a typical suburb that wanted to play city.

The hotel was easily the third-tallest building in the area, only bested by a ten-story office building and what appeared to be a downtown parking garage. I'd been to small towns in the past, but this was troubling compared to the hype this event drew online. I didn't think this little hamlet was ready for our bullshit. It was a quaint little town, just outside any of the major cities. Breezeway Acres sounded like an apartment complex more than a township. Either way, they had a Hilton property, and I was about that life. Gold Status, baby.

I parked at the Hampton Inn. Nothing too fancy, just some topiary lining the parking lot and a modest number of spaces for no more than fifty cars. Overflow parking was in the Bob Evans across the street, I'd imagine. If it wasn't overflow, it was surely my destination for breakfast. It had been a while since I had some breakfast down on the farm. You know, the chain restaurant farm.

I snagged my luggage from the trunk and wheeled toward the check-in desk. The kid behind the counter seemed less the hotel manager type and more the frontman for an emo band.

"Checking in?" he asked.

I glanced at his nametag. "Absolutely, Keith." I handed him my ID card.

He reached for my card, and a wall of sleeve tattoos came flying at me from above his wrist, casually hidden beneath a button-down collared shirt.

"You in a band?" I asked.

"Oh," Keith said, looking at his arm, smoothing out the cuff. "Yeah, actually. You like screamcore?"

I stared at him and gently smiled. I think my expression gave it away.

"My band is like Senses Fail, Blessthefall, or Black Veil Brides."

My eyes perked up at Keith. "I know some of those bands!"

Keith handed me my ID and slipped something on top of my card.

"What's this?" I asked, holding a business card adorned with a weird QR code, as I put my ID into my wallet.

"Oh. Well, I'm not supposed to actually do that, but you seem like a cool dude. It's the link to my band's music. Stream it when you get a chance and let me know what you think."

I flipped the card over a few times. "Do I just scan this thing with my phone?"

"You can do that or just look us up. It all goes to the same place in the end." Keith handed my room key card to me. "Third floor, left at the snack machine."

I held up the cards in a show of thanks and dragged my suitcase behind me to the elevator. I had no issue talking to people about anything, and life was all about networking. You never knew who you'd know until you knew them, right?

The lift ride was smooth, and the room was beautiful—beautiful by three-star hotel standards, at least. I always enjoyed getting to the events a day early. It gave me time to decompress, to relax, and to get my head right. I also had this high hope of writing my books while on these trips. I'd always ensure the hotel contained a writing desk or an office space of sorts for me to work in. What would start as a plan to write the next groundbreaking novel often turned into me watching *Monarch* on Apple TV or another binge of *King of the Hill* on Hulu. Lately, my distraction was *What We Do in the Shadows*. I was just a regular human writer, just writing regular human books. If I would actually pen some words, that is.

I set up my laptop on the desk and hung my button-up Hawaiian shirts. My tradition when traveling was never to unpack more than that, so why start now? I inventoried my necessities, and as I was double checking the underwear and socks, my phone buzzed violently on the bed. The screen read, BRIAN.

"Yo!" I said.

"Hey, it's Brian."

"I know. Where you at, man? You in town? It's pushing dinnertime, and I didn't want to just dine alone, as usual."

"I'm thirty out. I'm down for some beers and maybe something to eat. Anyone else in town?"

I paused. I hadn't texted anyone else to see who was in town. "Want me to send a message to a few folks to see about meeting up somewhere? Anywhere in mind?"

I heard some commotion on Brian's end.

"What was that?" I asked.

"Oh, that's just Callie and Marissa being loud again."

"You guys carpooled again? You brave man."

"Harry, you're on speakerphone, by the way."

"Caw-Cawl!" I heard the girls belt out—a great inside joke that will never die.

"Caw!" I called back through my phone.

"Well, the girls have been antsy to get out of the car and stretch legs, so after we get to the hotel and get situated, I'll hit you up," Brian said as the girls made a lot of noise in the background.

"I'll see if Dan or Barrios are here yet," I said and looked at my phone to send messages.

"Cool. You do that. I'll call you soon. Catch you later, bud."

Brian disconnected, and an eerie silence fell on my room. It was clear to me that our collective presence at any bar that had the misfortune of hosting us would instantly end the silence. I sent a quick message to Barrios and Dan, letting them know I was in town early and will probably be up for drinks soon.

The three telltale dots of Barrios's pending message appeared instantly. He was often quick to reply. *Thanks for the offer, but we'll be in early on Friday. Maybe drinks on Friday, too?*

I remained on unread status from Dan, assuming he was driving or was busy.

For a minute, I scanned my Google Maps, the images of various restaurants blurring together before I closed my eyes, the faint glow of the phone easing me into a half-sleep.

CHAPTER 8

*"Don't you blame the movies.
Movies don't create psychos. Movies
make psychos more creative!"*

— *Billy Loomis,* Scream

My phone convulsed on my chest, jolting me awake. For a split second, I forgot where I was, who I was, and what I was doing. Reaching for the phone, I gathered my surroundings and glanced at the screen. Four missed texts and three missed calls. I had apparently been out like a corpse. I hit the last incoming contact name to return the numerous missed calls from Brian. He'd been calling for nearly an hour.

"You live!"

"I live, much to the surprise of my enemies. They try," I joked.

"We're at a steakhouse down the street, if you're wanting to join. It's called Ray's Steaks and More."

The *more* concerned me, honestly. Just call it a steakhouse and be done. I knew what was in there. It was pretty cut and dry. Well, I hoped when I cut the meat it wasn't dry.

"Give me like ten minutes to put on my face, and I'll search it up."

I hung up with Brian and tossed the phone to the other side of the bed. I convulsed in a mini fit, trying to get my blood pumping enough to get out of bed. By the time I had gotten my shoes on and headed for the door, I was as awake as I was going to be. The elevator ride was shaky but nothing noteworthy. I punched in the steakhouse and more's name into my phone, and it popped up almost instantly. I felt a rush of relief when I found out the place was only six minutes from the hotel. I pushed Navigate and hopped into my car.

The steakhouse's façade was as expected. Partially because Google had spoiled its decor for me. Wooden front, like a shack or a cabin, which was clearly just a decorative front for typical modern-day construction. The interior looked like someone had tried to rebuild a Texas Roadhouse from memory. The air smelled of an assault of ten thousand aromas all at once. It wasn't unpleasant, just a lot for the senses.

"Harry!!!!!" a voice yelled from the dining area.

I waved, trying to decipher who it was. I had to wear glasses, but I was also stubborn enough to never wear them. It was Brian, surrounded by the other misfit authors, Callie and Marissa. They were goofing around with straw wrappers by the time I sat. It hadn't been three seconds before I took a blown wrapper to the cheek.

"Got him!" Callie yelled, high-fiving Marissa.

I looked at Brian, who just shrugged. "Kids, am I right?"

Marissa slugged Brian's arm.

"Speaking of kids"—Brian eyed his daughter sitting next to him—"Analise is joining us this weekend."

Analise turned beet red as Brian stood to offer applause, as if she were a guest of honor and had just received an award. "Analise, ladies and gentlemen."

Brian always did a great job of being that loud dad. He was obnoxious, loved to intentionally embarrass his kids, and absolutely relished the fact he genuinely embarrassed them. Analise had been the first to figure out that he would go out of his way to act as *dad-like* as possible—trying to use the wrong words, misspeaking phrases, and doing things over the top. She had learned years ago to stop saying, "I'm hungry," because the inevitable follow up was *Hungry* being greeted by Dad. Analise awkwardly half waved to the table as she sat next to her father.

"So, anything new?" Brian asked me.

"I fixed the handrail in the back yard leading to the basement," I said, staring at the menu.

Brian grabbed a straw and shot me with the wrapper. "No, dummy. I meant with your book."

I surveyed the items listed under the *Hores Devour* section. The typo nagged at me.

"Well?" Brian prodded.

"I don't know what I'm going to order. This is a massive menu, and it's got typos everywhere!" I said.

"Aaaay, just like your books," Analise interjected, and Brian glared at her with pursed lips.

I studied a menu item called *Mediterranean Leave Arrangement WITH a Buttermilk Aioli Drizzle*. I assumed they were trying to tell me that it was a salad with *leaves* and ranch dressing. This place tried too hard where it didn't matter.

"Earth to Harry," Marissa yelled, tapping her glass with a fork.

"Oh, what now?" I glanced up from the erratically punctuated and mispronounced menu.

"How's the new book?" Brian asked. "I only asked you fifty years ago."

I stared for a moment. "Well, I don't know. I can't figure out anything to really get it going, and it's bothering me."

"Get it going? How so?" Callie asked.

"It's the process. I just need to have a good crux to the story, and I can't figure out any decent characters. I just need something to inspire a spark or something," I said, glancing back at the menu.

"How's Violet? I know there was some stuff going down," Brian said.

"Stuff going down?" Marissa asked, sitting upright. "What stuff?"

"She okay?" Callie asked.

"Sure. Just knocked the shit out of some bully at school. Nothing too out of character for her."

"That's my girl." Brian raised a hand for a high-five that no one returned.

"Audrey isn't having it, though. She's been stressed about the whole thing." My gaze scanned more pretentious menu choices for a restaurant that absolutely should not be this fancy.

The table resumed a slow roar of noise, with everyone's conversations carrying across the place settings. The cacophony was enough to draw the waiter to our location.

"I see everyone is here," the man said in a condescending tone.

"Can I put a drink in?" I surveyed the assortment of mixed drinks, beers, and one orange soda. "Coke, please."

"Absolutely." The waiter eyed me for a moment, then faced the rest of the table. "Are we ready to order?"

"If you're ready, I'm ready," Brian said, closing the menu.

I shrugged. I figured, at best, I'd panic order. One by one, everyone gave their order. Marissa picked some meal apart until it was so customized it didn't resemble anything from the menu. The dreaded moment came. I sat, checking emails and texts on my phone, rather than order from the menu. The waiter, Tyron—as his tag indicated—hovered over me with his pad and pen.

I glanced around the restaurant for inspiration in the three seconds I had. "I see the special is chicken cordon bleu. I'm a sucker for chicken cordon bleu. How is that?"

"It's the special, so it's pretty popular," Tyron said. I couldn't read if he was being sarcastic.

"Can I get it without the broccoli? Can I substitute it with something else? Like corn, maybe?" I asked, laying down the menu.

"Corn? I can ask the chef, but they rarely alter the special."

Tyron closed his notepad, collected the menus from everyone, and bopped over to the kitchen.

"Look at you, mister adventurous. The cordon bleu. Fancy, now?" Brian joked.

I raised an eyebrow and squinted at him, and the girls resumed their loud discussion about some of the event guests attending alongside us. Brian interjected a handful of times, while I tuned out the noise to thumb through social media on my phone. Flipping through article after article, I was bored, looking for anything to keep my attention.

I had been so involved with my mindless activities that I didn't notice my Coke had appeared on the table. I quickly tossed the straw into the glass and took a large sip.

"So, what time do we want to get in there tomorrow?" Brian asked. "They open at ten in the morning, but I'm not feeling that gung-ho."

"Maybe two o'clock? Gives us time to hit the mall and maybe even hit that museum downtown," Callie suggested.

"I could hit a mall," I added.

As we were deep in discussion, I caught what I assumed was the chef leaning out from the swinging kitchen door. "He wants the corn?" the chef yelled to Tyron.

"Yeah, the corn," Tyron responded from the drink station, filling another customer's beverage.

"The. Corn," the chef asked once more for clarification.

"What's with the corn? Is it that strange of a choice?" I asked the table.

"I had a corny joke here, but I'll save that for later when you get 'The. Corn.' with your extra fancy meal," Brian said, laughing.

I always left myself open for moments like this. It was never intentional, but we will be talking about this corn for a while, I guess. I resumed my scrolling, but our meals came sooner than expected. I scrutinized my special, including the very bright yellow corn. This stuff looked like it had been steeping inside a radioactive barrel from *Return of the Living Dead*. I ate the cordon bleu, picked at the corn that I so desperately had to have, and ate the dry mashed potatoes. This event weekend was shaping up to be wonderful already.

We finished eating, and Brian picked up today's tab, under the pretense that tomorrow would be my problem, and the girls would tag in for the weekend outings. It was the best way to do things, and we never went too wild, out of respect. Except for that time Marissa ordered four strawberry daiquiris by accident. We had to carry her out that night.

We stood in the parking lot, enjoying the wonderful chilly air.

"See you in the afternoon?" Brian asked.

"We meeting for lunch prior to loading in?" I asked.

The girls chanted in unison. "MALL! MALL! MALL! MALL!"

Brian added to the fray with the chant, echoing "Mall" right with them.

I raised my hand to silence the angry mob. "Okay, mall around noon? Shop, eat, and pop into the convention center to set up and sell?"

"Sounds good. Look, as much as I'd love to sit out here and be an absolute further nuisance to the restaurant, it's frigging cold out here," Brian shivered out.

I was far more tolerant of the cold. Honestly, most harsh conditions really didn't bother me, aside from absurd amounts of heat. The girls didn't say the same, but they showed they were cold. Analise was already reaching for her dad's keys to start the car.

"Okay, I'll catch you guys tomorrow," I said and approached my car.

We all split ways, turning different directions toward our accommodations. I set the GPS to head to mine.

FRIDAY

"Oh, it's night time. I was having a daymare."

-Dracula, Dracula Dead and
Loving It

CHAPTER 9

"If you are the killer, that's cool, just, you know, don't kill me!"

— *Dave,* Club Dread

Everything was on fire. I couldn't rip off the blankets fast enough. My laptop provided enough ambient light as I leaped out of bed. Calmly, yet swiftly, I sauntered to the bathroom. I took a knee and proceeded to pray to the gods of the porcelain. My head spun and ached, my stomach felt awful, and my body heat was out of control. I spewed several huge stomachfuls of today's meals into the toilet. Nothing but the faint nightlight came from the outlet on the wall to illuminate the room.

Once the waves of sick settled, I turned on the light. The toilet glowed a neon yellow. I blew my nose as I looked in horror. *The. Corn.*

"Shoulda known something was up with that corn," I said as I flushed the toilet.

To feel cleaner, I swished some mouthwash in my mouth. My head pounded, and I felt awful. The room spun slightly and had shifted from the pits of hell to the frozen tundra. My body temperature was in flux. The room whirled violently as I collapsed onto the bed, a dizzying wave engulfing me. I attempted to turn on the hotel television and switch through stations, until I landed on a made-for-TV version of the *Avengers* film. I couldn't even focus on the screen.

I retrieved a washrag from the bathroom, soaked it in cold water, and placed it on my head as I lay back down. I needed off this ride. This was not how I had planned to start my weekend at Nightmares Unbound. What a great first impression, to show up completely drained of color and puking my brains out with food poisoning. I found the energy to snag my phone to check the time—2:15 a.m. Likely I was opting out of mall and lunch adventures in favor of sleeping in as late as possible. I listened to quips from Iron Man as I drifted into sleep.

I awoke almost on the hour for the next two hours, unloading my stomach contents a handful of times. Almost desperately, I chugged water to fill myself with something to help remove the tainted corn. After another few kneeling exercises, I felt I was finally empty. I returned slowly to the bed and placed the cold rag back on my head. I fell asleep to the sounds of the Hulk smashing everything. What a soothing lullaby, coupled with the hum of the air conditioning kicking up.

My alarm screamed at me, with Marc Rebillet saying to "Get the Fuck out of Bed, Bitch." Normally I'd wake with a smile, but today I was dead on arrival. I slapped for the snooze button on my phone. The room's darkening shades were doing their job, because it still seemed like midnight. Fumbling for my phone, I saw it was 9:00 a.m. The television must have turned off automatically, or in my nauseated stupor, I had shut it down. In either case, the only light was a sliver creeping around the curtains and my cellphone.

My head hurt, and I felt awful. I didn't feel sick anymore, just felt like I had taken part in a fight club, and I was here to talk about it. My muscles ached, but I didn't feel as bad as last night. Nothing would feel that bad. I pushed myself to climb from the king bed and pulled back the curtain a bit to reveal the scenic view of the parking lot. The world was alive with activity.

I showered and dressed while *Bluey* played on the television behind me. It was my ritual, and regardless of if I felt like hammered shit, why break tradition? I checked my phone after putting on my shoes. The group text chat was on fire. I'd missed at least forty messages or more. I hastily thumbed through dozens of memes, including the absurd amount of poorly photoshopped Brian-as-Wonder-Woman photos. I clearly had missed something big.

Meet in the empty Sears parking lot by 1140. Food court is right next to it.

I tuned in for the last leg of the episode of *Bluey*. The family was discussing the dad blowing a fart at one of the kids' faces, while he denied it. Using his defense, "Whoever smelled it, dealt it," I chuckled a bit. I grabbed my electronics, chargers, and necessities and tossed them into my shoulder bag. I was ready to go from the restaurant to the convention center. Before I closed the door, I checked the room one last time.

The lobby smelled like a breakfast disaster. Overwhelming scents of coffee, bacon, eggs, waffles, and more hit me like a heavyweight boxer. My stomach informed me that I better not try it, but I guess it didn't get the memo that we were headed for food. I maneuvered through the continental breakfast, snagging a muffin and a cup of Coke. I sat on a stool and slowly tested the waters with eating. After a few moments, I felt like I was good enough to take on the world. After last night, anything crazy with set up should feel like cake.

CHAPTER 10

Nightmares Unbound Promotional Poster

By the time I headed to the mall, it was nearly noon—that allotted little time for shopping and screwing off.

With more potholes than parking spaces, the parking lot was in terrible condition. No one had repainted those lines for as long as I'd been alive, most likely. The mall's façade left something to be desired, trapped in a limbo that lived between the eighties and the nineties and wasn't sure which one it wanted to be. In either case, both decades were a half-assed amalgamation of this excuse for a mall.

I thought it was bad outside until I pulled the single-working entrance door. The handicapped button didn't even automatically open it, which I felt was in poor taste. That should have been something they at least pretended to care about, guys. The smell of stale rugs, the stench of a ham sandwich—which I could only assume was not, in fact, a ham sandwich—and a cross between neon and halogen lighting, half of which were not even working, greeted me when I entered the mall.

I tried to find a mall directory, but in my haste to do so, I stumbled upon the food court. It sported an Asian bistro, an Auntie Anne's Pretzels, and the forever mall staple, Sbarro. I spotted Brian and the gang down the end of the hall in front of El Ubicación, which I assumed was a Mexican joint. Given that my wife was Hispanic and that I had spent a good amount of time in the Southwest and that I had mildly paid attention in my shabby high school Spanish class, I think it should have been spelled *La* Ubicación. But what do I know?

"There he is!" Brian's voice echoed through the desolate mall.

I looked around as if someone far more important was behind me before walking to join them.

"Sorry, this place had strawberry daiquiris, and you know Marissa." Brian motioned toward the red cups in front of our fellow author friend.

"Howdy, gang!" Marissa said, clearly consuming one daiquiri too many already.

I surveyed the food, which appeared relatively edible but nothing special. My stomach flipped before I opted out to see what the food court had in store for me later. "I'm good on the whole *eating* thing. I'll just be here for moral support while you guys have at it."

Brian cocked his head and squinted at me in disappointment. "Chip? Salsa? May I offer you a Wonka Bar, for that elusive golden ticket?"

I chortled and shook my head at Brian's ability to always find a way to shoehorn in some reference to one of his favorite films, but I also didn't know how much to trust my stomach after it had warred with me last night. That was what I got for having *the corn* from a sketchy restaurant. Brian inched the small bowl of queso toward me. I reluctantly reached for a chip and tried a bit. It stayed down, so I figured I'd take a chance with a few more.

"You look like Death's cousin's college roommate paid you a visit," Brian said.

"I feel like it."

"I didn't want to say anything," Callie said and shoved a loaded chip into her maw.

I finished chewing the last bit of chip and swallowed. "I had a bit of a run in last night with *the corn.*"

Brian smirked a bit. "He wants *the corn?*"

I wiped the cheese from my face. "I should have known to take heed when there was an entire congressional debate about the status of *the corn* at my expense."

Marissa finished a long chug of her daiquiri. "It was glowing, my guy."

I admit, this was a fact. The corn was radioactive. The expelled corn had been like a Chernobyl experiment from a horror movie at ground zero. It had been luminous. I didn't even need to turn on the bathroom light to see it.

Brian pushed away his plate of beans and rice and tossed his napkin into the fray. "I think that's about the end of the line for me."

Marissa finished the rest of her drink. Callie was a bit more discrete and placed her silverware crisscrossed onto her plate. The waitress noticed we were ready to go and rushed the check to the table.

"To go?" the waitress pointed to the drink in front of Marissa.

"Don't threaten her with a good time. No, we're good," Brian said, presenting his bank card.

The waitress returned quickly, we headed toward the exit.

"So, you joined us just to have a few scoops of cheese and a sip of water or two?" Brian jested.

I reflected on that for a moment. "Yeah, I guess so. I should have just stayed in the room to recover some more."

Once in the parking lot, we divided up toward our respective two vehicles, and I realized I had parked nowhere near them.

"See you there?" I yelled.

Brian tossed me a thumbs-up. Callie let out a loud "CAW-CAW" over the hum of the generators and traffic.

I retrieved my phone and let my GPS app navigate to the convention center's address. It was a few minutes from here, which I was happy for. The hard part was here. It was time to load in my thousands of pounds full of books. I climbed into my car and started toward the Civic Center.

CHAPTER 11

"Don't open that door!"

— *Albert Wesker,* Resident Evil

The building was massive. The parking garage was housed underneath the main building. According to the website, there was ample parking for us *and* the attendees. As I approached, I noticed the parking space indicator system showed ten floors of parking underground. Thousands of spots were shown in green LED text next to each floor. This thing was a behemoth. I'd done events in DC, and even in Philly, and none of their centers rivaled this one. New construction let them get away with a lot.

The Brentworth Center was new. I think they put it together in the past decade, maybe less. It had all the newest amenities, including fast internet, a wonderful food court for concessions, and ample power capabilities for plugging in all our stupid devices. I don't even think the carpet had been worn in yet. As I pulled in, I was greeted by an attendant.

A stout yet balding attendant, with DOUG on his nametag, greeted me as I entered. "Hey there! Here for the convention?" Cheerful, Doug either loved his job or could fake it with the best of them.

"Absolutely, Doug," I replied with enthusiasm. "I'm actually one of the guests. Do we park somewhere special or just wherever is open?"

Doug thought for a moment. "I wasn't given guidance on that one, but I can check." He stepped away and radioed someone, then nodded a few times as a buzzing voice responded to him. After a few confirmations and head shakes, he reapproached. "Nope. It's fair game. Wild West! I do recommend parking on the fourth or fifth floors, since they're the easiest to get in and out of. Anything lower and you'll have to take the center access ramps. Four and five use the perimeter ramps, which route almost directly here.

They spit you out on the second floor, and it's less of a wait come Sunday if you're leaving then."

I looked ahead at the garage. "That sounds good, man. I appreciate ya."

When the hell did I start saying, "I appreciate ya?"

Doug gave a gentle tap on my car's roof and pressed the button to raise the garage gate arm. I drove in, scanning for anything that signified the fourth floor's location.

It didn't take long to find a parking spot on the fourth floor. I was in lot A4, which I joked how the font made it resemble *Ah*—the element-of-surprise lot. Spanish Inquisition lot. Nobody expected this lot! I should remember that come tonight. I snagged a photo of it regardless, because I knew I'd forget it by the time I reached the elevator.

I quickly loaded my wagon and was on my way. I followed the confusing maze of stairs and elevator signs, which pointed me in different directions. I was thankful I had bought the new cart before this event. It held nearly four hundred pounds of weight, and I felt like my books were double that. In reality, it was probably closer to a hundred pounds. It wove easily around each corner, following me as I made my path toward the lifts.

I heard a familiar sound—the BOOP of an elevator arriving at a floor. I rounded the next turn and passed through lot 19h, before seeing the silver doors. Luckily, it took only a moment to get to me. I wheeled in, careful not to let the doors smash my wagon as they closed. The floor *M* was the longest button. According to the guide above the buttons, that stood for MAIN. I guess that was where I was headed. The emails were vague enough.

The elevator ride was smooth. I went up what felt like fifty floors, but it was more like five. Giant silver doors peeled open to reveal a bustling lobby that filed into a larger show floor. The floors were unscuffed. The paint and wallpaper were fresh, and the lights were brand new. This place hadn't been used since its construction. I highly doubted someone had even shit in the atrium yet. I followed the signs to the vendor check-in.

A lovely little blonde girl greeted me at the table. "Name?" she asked, barely looking up from stacks of printed spreadsheets.

"Oh, I'm a guest author. I could be on that list, but I see this one labeled *Guests*. Wanted to save the trouble."

"Thanks. No one really does that. Let me see." She reached for the list labeled *Special Guests*. "I see a handful of names. I just need your ID."

I passed her my driver's license and waited patiently. She scanned page after page. I assumed it was alphabetical, which usually put me at the front of the line. Who knows what they did here.

"Okay, Harry. Your table is number 1704. You'll just head in straight, until you hit the giant pole, turn left in the main aisle. From there, go that way for a bunch of aisles, until you see seventeen hundred. Turn right, and your booth is eight in from the wall."

The girl made it sound so simple. I expected to take at least ten trips around that giant pole before I figured myself out. By the sixth time around, I'd be joking in my best Chevy Chase voice, *"Look kids, parliament. Big Ben!"*

I took my badges and wandered confusedly through the large doors. Everything about this room felt sterile—clean and white everywhere. Signs hung from the ceiling to denote aisles and location. The doors were few and far between, save for a fire exit or two. It appeared the brunt of the traffic would funnel through the very doors I had entered through. I kept wheeling my way along.

I arrived at the large pillar in the center. It really made no sense to even have it, with a building this immense. Was this the central support beam to hold it all together? I turned left and navigated through the sea of tables. I noticed several vendors had already set up their tables yesterday or had gotten an early start today. I saw the numbers above my head and kept pushing forward.

Any natural lighting wasn't even a thing in here. This place seemed to just be a giant warehouse. I looked up as I went under the numbers.

1400.

1500.

1600.

1700. I was here. I turned and wandered down the aisle. Using the wall as a starting point, I counted upward and read the names displayed on the open tables. I saw a few that I recognized.

"Ooh, Dan is here? And so is Barrios? This is the party aisle now!"

I found my table. It was a big booth for me, and I felt like I should have brought more things to fill the space. I was here. This was the start of a long weekend. I had only a few scant hours to set myself up and take my first lap around this monstrosity of a convention.

CHAPTER 12

Chibi Design by Cailin

My signs and books went up in a breeze. I had so much room that I didn't feel like I was stacked onto myself or fighting for space. I'd vended at conventions that gave us less than two feet between me and the booth behind me. This place had easily twenty feet between me and the vendor behind me. So much room for activities!

I withdrew the paper map that the front desk had handed me. It was already sweaty and getting a bit gross. I searched for Brian and the gang but didn't see them in my aisle. I wandered to the 1400s. Brian's corner booth was empty; I wondered how the hell I had beaten them here so easily.

"Hey, buddy!" I heard from behind me.

I whirled around to see Cailin, an artist friend of mine for years. She'd done a few designs for a Chibi version of me for keychains and stickers. I didn't even know what that meant, but I can tell you that Cartoon Harry was adorable, covered in blood, with a knife and giant blue anime eyes. She had a way with art, that was for sure. We met ages ago when her wife and I sang karaoke at an afterparty. I was a sucker for singing, and if a stranger approached you, dressed as an alligator to sing "Crocodile Rock," well, you fucking do it.

"Hey! Been a while!" I took a hug from her. "Where are they hiding you out here?"

Cailin vaguely gestured to the monstrous open building. "Somewhere in the nine hundreds. I was just running to get a water, and I spotted you."

"Oh, dope. Well, I'm over there in the seventeens I think."

"Well, it was good seeing you. I'm going to get that water before I can't ever leave my booth again. I'd end up dying in here."

"Nobody wants that." I laughed as Cailin wandered toward the concession area.

I continued to tour the layout. A few hours before the event opened, and it never ceased to amaze me how many people would set up at the absolute last minute. I hoped my booth neighbor wouldn't show so I could shove Brian and the gang into where I was, or vice versa. It was a little strange not to feature the guests and the talent in a single area. Not my rodeo, not my monkeys.

I wandered through at least a dozen aisles before I felt like I might die. After I finished browsing the Manga booth that sold replica swords and Godzilla merch, I meandered to my booth. I ascended the aisle numbers once more before realizing I didn't have a drink. I detoured to the concessions for the biggest bottle of Coke I could muster.

"They just let anybody in here, don't they?" I heard from behind.

I turned around. "Sawney frigging Hatton. The only guy I know whose name sounds like he's been feuding with his neighbors for four hundred years. How's it going?"

"Can't complain. Did you see how massive this place is? It's almost unnecessarily big. Where did they stick you?"

"Seventeen something. I think I'm right at the end of one of the rows, maybe oh-four or oh-five. You'll know it when you see my banner."

"Sweet. I'm not too far off. Somewhere in the nineteens. I'll come pester you about the new book later this weekend."

I smirked. "What new book?"

"Oh, damn. Still? Well, I came out with a new one a few months ago that I hope goes over well here."

I grabbed my soda from the concession attendant. "Well, I wish the best for you. I hope you leave with an empty box."

"Better to leave *with* one than *in* one, right?" Sawney joked as he stepped forward to order.

"Okay, man. Catch you later," I said and headed toward my booth.

I was excited to see so many familiar faces. Something was comforting about being in a sea of uncharted newness yet seeing a handful of people I knew and who I got along with. I resumed sitting at my booth and people-watched as everyone trickled in to set up their tables and displays.

One by one, the displays came to life. Brilliant colors, posters, and banners filled the aisle around me as authors, artists, and other creatives set up their wares. Across from me was a person who turned decrepit old shopworn books into beautiful floral arrangements. Diagonal from me sat an artist who did horror interpretations of classic Disney and Nickelodeon characters. I knew I'd be fighting myself to resist the urge to buy *The Walking Dead* and *The Wild Thornberrys* crossover. He would get a sale by Sunday, for certain.

"Attention esteemed guests and vendors! This is Benjamin Parker here, officially welcoming you to what we hope to be the East Coast's biggest horror festival, if not the entire United States!" a voice boomed across the PA system and through the cavernous building.

"Mayfield here. I hope everyone has a truly bloody good time!"

An audible *POP* resounded with each click of the mic whenever the speaker fired up. I figured they'd sort that out later, likely only realizing the PA issue now. After I relaxed back into my chair, my phone buzzed. It was Brian, letting me know the gang was in, badged, and all set up. The event was surely filling out to be something insane.

CHAPTER 13

"In the midst of chaos, there is also opportunity."

— *Sun Tzu,* The Art of War

grew tired of waiting. I checked my watch and saw an hour remained before the event officially started. One thing I liked to do was to peek outside to see what everyone was doing. Were there cool costumes? Any fans of my work? Not that I'd know, but a guy can dream. I trekked toward the entrance.

Once I was outside, a line like no other greeted me. Adults, kids, and everything in between lined the side of the building. This was a weekday! Unprecedented! I went live on my phone and streamed to all my social media. I ran up and down to get video of the wild costumes as I got everyone hyped. It wasn't my job, but it was something I loved to do. Folks cheered, threw up horns and peace signs, waved, and more. A hell of a reaction. I directed my viewers to come down and check it out.

I'd never heard such a pop before. It got me excited as I returned to my table. I told everyone to come find my book, and I hoped at least one of them did. I floated to my booth with adrenaline. What felt like an eternity to walk went by in a breeze, and I nearly missed hearing Brian call for me.

"Harry! Where the hell are you going? Can't say hi?" Brian yelled at me.

I beheld his setup. Several Hugo nominations. An Oprah Book Club pick. It made my table, covered in bloody weapons and a dead bird decoration from the dollar store, look like child's play. I really needed to write things that were full of substance. Brian was over here, churning out world-changing work, and I was writing a story about a toaster that became a cop, 100 percent a rip-off of my favorite '80's flick. Between that and my B-movie script about my time in the military, fighting alien monsters, I wasn't exactly getting on Oprah's list.

"Look at you, fancy pants!" I said jokingly.

"I got a few new banners since the last event. Figured this would be a good time to debut the Oprah sign."

"Look under your chairs! You get Brian's book! You get Brian's book! Everybody gets his books!" I belted out in my best Oprah impression.

"Bravo," Brian said, giving a slow clap. "Are you done?"

"Probably, but we'll just have to see. The night is still young."

I helped Brian hang his last banner and got some things turned on and plugged in. He most recently debuted a novel where he had spent weeks inside an insane asylum that the state had decommissioned decades ago. He was a better man than me, because I didn't care how lucrative the book deal was. It would take a lot of arm twisting and convincing to get me to spend twenty minutes in there.

"It's about to open soon. You better get back to your booth," Brian said, gazing at his phone.

I checked my watch. "As if I'd worry anyone by me actually being at my booth. It's normal to never see me."

Brian and I fist bumped as I turned to begin the walk toward my row.

"Dinner at the burger joint tonight?" Brian yelled.

I threw a thumbs-up over my head without looking back.

"THE CONVENTION WILL OPEN IN TEN MINUTES!"

The voice echoed through the aisles of the festival. I thought to myself how similar it was to the Purge announcement. I passed a ton of great art, including someone who made beautiful Japanese rice scrolls of famous cartoon characters, almost causing me to spend the money on a samurai Hank Hill design.

By the time I had reached my table, the crowds were descending the stairs, elevators and escalators. Even for a Friday, the sheer volume of people flooding in was overwhelming; a cacophony of sounds and movement filled the space. I immediately went to work, and within minutes, I already had a dozen people lined up for me to sign their copies of my books or to purchase a new one.

"I really loved the one about the guy with the lawnmower," one person said.

"Are these really based on true stories?" another puzzled.

"You're my favorite writer," one said, clearly unaware of any other authors in the world.

"Hey, can you tell me about this one?" A man pointed toward my science-fiction novel.

I gave him the rundown of the plot as best I could. He seemed spacy and distant.

"And this one here? What is your favorite one in this short-story collection?"

Again, I spent a few minutes explaining the story's core elements and plot progression, carefully avoiding any major spoilers. It was a hard thing to do, but I want to keep it interesting without revealing the crux of the story.

"Oh, cool. Thanks for regaling me with your tales. I don't have any money, though." The man took a curt bow, tipped his imaginary hat, and exited down the aisle.

After several exhausting hours of signing books, pitching synopsis, and explaining the books to what felt like hundreds of people, I finally got a break at 8 p.m.

"You've been crazy busy, man," a voice said from across my table.

I looked up from my book rack to see Barrios—dressed in a dark wizard outfit, his naturally frizzy curly hair exploded into a cloud of chaos to add to the outfit, with a shaggy beard to match—venture across the aisle to talk.

"That's impressive, dude."

"Surprisingly, yes, and it's only Friday!" I said.

Fridays were typically the slower days. We would muddle through Friday so we could get into the meat of the busy day, which was always Saturday. Everyone was off work and longing for something fun to do. With the assortment of authors, special guests, and activities, how could one not attend?

"Book count is three for me."

My gaze fell upon Barrios. I remembered the three-book-sale events. Hell, I remembered the zero-book-sale events from the early days of my career. "Three is solid, dude. Hell yeah! Not bad for a Friday."

Barrios smirked. "I guess you're right. It just bummed me out a bit."

I nodded, doing my best to reassure him that some days were better than others. As I fished for my next thought, my phone buzzed in my back pocket. I reached for it, and Barrios took his leave. The call was from my wife. Audrey had the unique privilege of being one of two people in my phone with backgrounds for their caller ID. Hers was of Gunter, the penguin from *Adventure Time*, playing piano, with the words FUCK YOU emblazoned over him. It was so fitting, and I chuckled every time I saw it.

"What's up?" I answered and noticed the aisles had died down fairly well for the moment.

"You need to get your child."

The voice on the other end did not sound pleased. And when Violet was *my child*, we knew this would not go well. I braced myself for the follow up.

"Could you take her for the weekend? I just spent the past two hours on the phone with her teacher. She's been acting out more than we thought. Plus, everyone called out of work tomorrow, and guess who gets to go in on their day off?"

I bit my tongue to not answer with a smartass comment for the rhetorical question. "So, what do you want me to do?"

"Which hotel are you staying at? Can I bring her by tonight?"

"Tonight?"

"Yes, tonight. I won't have time in the morning. She'll probably pass out asleep before I pull up to the front doors."

I could tell Audrey already had Violet's bags packed and halfway into the car. My sixth sense tingled; I wasn't saying no to this one.

"The event ends in two hours. That should be just enough time to bring her my way. We're going to dinner though. Think she'll find energy to do that?" I asked, sitting in my chair behind my booth.

"Vi! You want dinner with Daddy?" Audrey screamed into the receiver, followed by Vi's excited squeals. "I guess she wants dinner. We'll load up her overnight bag and head your way. Text me the hotel address."

I must have audibly sighed. Audrey picked up on it faster than a bloodhound around piece of dropped turkey on Thanksgiving.

"Just call me when you're in the area, and I'll figure out the rest. I shouldn't be long leaving here. I'll let Brian and the gang know. He's picking up Analise from the hotel, since she wanted to veg out and watch terrible horror movies." I checked my watch. "I'd imagine that won't take him longer than it will for our exchange."

Violet yelled in excitement over the phone. Audrey could barely get a few words out. "Thanks, I owe you. I know she'll be a handful to keep an eye on at the event. We'll head out now. See you soon. Love you."

"Love you, too."

The phone disconnected, and I was once again thrust back into the reality of being at the convention. Surprisingly, it was trafficked but fairly dead by all rights. I spotted the one or two stragglers traversing my aisle alongside small families dressed as Art the Clown or wearing competing convention shirts to show they'd been to a different con and that they support the brand. I doubted I would sell another book.

I admired the artwork on the hanging signs. I wondered who did their convention art. Was it someone here, or was it an outside source? Then I noticed the abundance of cameras tacked to every pillar and column as far as I could see. There wasn't a blind spot in the joint. Big Brother really was watching, weren't they? With the uptick in public violent attacks, it was a reasonable measure. Between that and the guards wanding everyone on the way in, this should be uneventful.

I stared into the abyss, awaiting the coveted announcement stating the convention would be closing in ten minutes. The booming voice was a welcomed sound to my ears, because I wasted no time packing up my electronics and other goodies and loading my backpack to begin the journey to the exit. I figured it best to text Brian on the way out, letting him know I'd be plus-one for this evening. It was going to be a long Saturday.

CHAPTER 14

"This situation has got eldritch coming out the ass."

— *Cpl Flynn Taggart,* DOOM *by Dafydd ab Hugh*

Brian understood what had gone down. The quick text of *I have a plus-one* seemed straightforward enough. I pulled into the front of the hotel and noticed my wife's SUV parked already. The vehicle was vacant, and I assumed they were in the lobby. I grabbed my electronics for the event, slung the bag onto my back, and started for the lobby.

"Daddy!" Violet screamed as she squealed her way across a tired lobby. For the hour that it was, this kid was full of energy. "Are we dinnering with Mr. Brian?"

I took a knee, looking my wife in the eye briefly, then refocused on Violet. "We are! Do you want to ride the elevator to the top? We can put your bag in the room."

"ELEVATOR! ELEVATOR! ELEVATOR!" Violet chanted as she marched around the lobby sofa with her bag dragging behind her.

"Thanks for this. I owe you," Audrey said.

"It's easier for me to keep an eye on her where I am than it is for you. It's not an issue. She can restock my books." I laughed as Violet still paraded around the chair with limitless energy. "It's the least *she* can do."

Audrey checked her phone. "I need to get back if I want to get enough sleep for work tomorrow. See you on Sunday night?"

I stared blankly. Any questions involving money, time, or dates were a blur to me. "Yes? Oh, right. The thing ends on Sunday. Should be home by eight."

Eventually the gears turned enough for everything to make sense. I checked my phone as well to verify the convention information.

"I'll be up here tomorrow around four to snag her. It's an hour or so from work. If I get out on time, I'll be there," Audrey said. "Should I just text you when I'm in the area?"

"Yes. Also, text Brian. You know how I am at an event. More eyes looking at their phones, the better. At least he could send over Marissa or Callie to poke me."

I hugged my wife, and she said goodbye to Violet. As soon as the revolving door ceased to spin, Violet calmed down entirely.

"We are riding the elevator now, yes?" she asked.

I nodded, fishing my room key from my pocket. I walked her to the elevators, but not before mouthing my apologies to the exhausted-looking receptionist. Violet took the key from my hand and activated the elevator. She dashed inside the first open lift, and I quickly followed.

"Which floor are we?"

"Three," I said. I wondered if Keith had the day off today. He seemed like a cool dude.

I watched Violet stare at the number pad for a few moments before I gestured toward the button that read *3*.

"I knew that!" she scoffed.

Once inside the hotel room, we dumped our belongings, and Violet took a grand tour of the luxury one-room suite. She thought the ironing board was classy, as was the luggage stand. To this day, I don't think I had ever used the luggage stand. I actually had to Google what the hell it was used for a few years ago—resting a bag on during unpacking to not dirty the bed. I let the kiddo stare in amazement at our super-high third-floor view, which overlooked an overhang full of trash and bird shit.

"Neat!" she said.

"Ready to grab food with Mr. Brian and the gang? Analise is there."

"Analise! She's my bestest friend," Violet belted out as she marched toward the front door.

I thought to myself I had a strange kid, but I also know it was good how expressive she was. Very assertive little brat sometimes, but I wouldn't have it any other way. We ambled toward the elevator as I texted Brian that we were on our way.

CHAPTER 15

*"The fear of blood tends to create
fear for the flesh."*

— Silent Hill

The restaurant was packed. I was thankful Marissa had called ahead for reservations. I approached the table and saw Barrios had also joined us, as well as Sawney and even Cailin. We were clearly a server's worst nightmare, with the number of us who circled the table. Violet immediately took the chair next to Analise.

"About time you got here," Brian joked.

"Did you have *the corn*?" Marissa laughed.

I knew I'd never live that down. I sat next to Barrios and quickly grabbed the menu. This place was a Tex Mex and Asian infusion restaurant. What a combo!

"We let the server know to come back in a few. Shouldn't be waiting long," Callie said.

I panned the menu while everyone engaged in small talk.

"Did you happen to watch any of the Mayfield Mayhem films?" Barrios interjected.

The table fell to a mild hush.

"Those movies are fu—I mean messed up," Sawney said, eyeing Violet.

"I watched the one where the family is in a motel, and a group of psychos torture them. It was messed up, and that's putting it lightly!" Cailin said. "I'm not into gross horror like that, but I wanted to know who this guy was."

"Is it that bad?" Callie asked.

"Woof," I breathed out.

"That bad, huh?" Callie replied.

Sawney sat forward. "I wrote a book about a dude who banged a space cat, and even *I* was taken aback. Let me just say that."

"I happened to watch the one from a few years ago called *Zoopocalypse*, and it was just so gritty and nasty. Animals just tearing into screaming people for the sake of shock value," Marissa contributed. "I stopped after the first fifteen minutes."

"Fifteen? That's a new record for you and horror," Brian joked.

Marissa smirked before regarding the waiter. We put in our orders and had a pleasant evening. Marissa ordering chocolate milk with whipped cream for some reason was the highlight of discussion for a while. The food was amazing. We even saved room for dessert, as they say. Violet tore into her hybrid mochi and fried ice cream. It sounded weird to me, but she absolutely enjoyed it. Before long, we had cleared our table and were in the parking lot. Violet yawned, and her blinks became longer and longer.

"Well, that's it for me, you party animals," Brian said, checking his phone.

"Eleven too late for you?" I asked.

"Okay, Mr. 'I don't sleep ever.' Some of us actually want to sleep before this thing starts tomorrow."

"Is it nine?" Sawney asked, fishing for his keys.

"Early entry is nine. Event proper is ten," Cailin added, tightening her hoodie.

Two or three of us groaned, knowing it would be a long day tomorrow. Nine in the morning all the way until eight at night? A thirteen-hour marathon. I figured we'd be dead by tomorrow night. Somehow we would have to dig in our heels and find the strength to make it to Sunday. This was what I always did, though. I'd bitch and moan about the length of the event, and by Monday, I'd be missing it. My friends, the excitement, and the environment would make the event go by so much faster.

Each of us packed into our respective cars. I don't know when Violet fell asleep on the ride to the hotel, but she was out like a rock. I had to carry her corpselike body, limp and unresponsive save for the occasional snore, through the lobby. The receptionist likely picked up on the change in my energy as I boarded the elevator—the slowness of my steps, the quiet sigh I let out, all screamed *bedtime*.

I carefully laid out tomorrow morning's outfits, and I ensured I properly placed Violet in the bed. I took a few moments to get myself together and unwound by watching another Mayfield film on my laptop, listening with my earbuds. This one was an early film, from almost seventeen years ago, simply named, *Found*. Most of his titles were a play on the plot, like something about an office or a subway station. This was such a vague title.

A young, blonde female victim stumbled upon two others before the killer descended upon them. The third girl tried to write HELP US in the sawdust-coated floor before meeting her demise. There was no thought in this, but I could see how folks clung to the visceral animalistic nature of the filming process Mayfield took.

After about twenty minutes of another so-called recording that the police had found, according to the splash text, I'd had enough of this madness. I powered down the laptop and passed out in the bed without disturbing Violet.

SATURDAY

"We're on an express elevator to hell, going down!"

— *Pvt Hudson,* Aliens

CHAPTER 16

'It strikes me profoundly that the world is more often than not a bad and cruel place."

—   Patrick Bateman, Bret Easton Ellis' American Psycho

Getting myself together was one thing. Getting Violet together? Another beast. Try to put stockings on a cat while it was on fire on a roller coaster. That was the easier of the two tasks between that and getting Violet dressed in the morning. To my surprise, she'd already hit the bathroom, had cleaned herself up, and was brushing her teeth. Who was this child, and where was the pod she had emerged from?

She waved to me and continued to brush. I stumbled awake, turning the television on to Disney. Bluey was playing, as was my morning tradition. Something about Dad getting takeout, I believe. Violet wrapped up in the bathroom and plopped down to watch cartoons. I showered, dressed, and snagged all of my electronics from their chargers.

We ventured to the hotel-provided breakfast. Violet grabbed six whole pancakes and an orange. I didn't stop her. Who was I to tell her that it was a bad idea? I poured a cup of some generic Special K-looking cereal and 2% milk. I finished fairly quickly as Violet munched on pancake number four. To my surprise, she only didn't finish the orange, which I could reconcile by bringing with us to the convention.

"You ready for a big day?" I asked.

Violet nodded.

"Mommy is coming to grab you in the afternoon so you don't have to stay there all day with me," I said before slurping up the milk in the bowl.

Violet pouted and harrumphed as she shoved one more bite of pancake into her face, then called it quits completely.

"What's the matter?" I asked.

Violet tapped her stomach. "Someone around here ate too much pancakes."

I glanced around the room. "Who would have done such a thing?"

Violet smiled and shrugged innocently. I checked my watch—8:30. We needed to get into the building before they opened.

Violet tried to get up from the table but knocked her unused syrup onto the booth. I groaned and hastily grabbed a wad of napkins to soak up the syrup explosion. Feeling our window of arriving on time closing with every tick, we rushed to the car. After being convinced we hit every red traffic light in the city while driving to the convention center, I turned into the garage.

A different sentry manned the gate, much younger and not as friendly. "Fifth floor, turn left for the parking." He offered me nothing further. No *"Good day, how you doin?"* or anything.

The gate lifted, and I pulled around and upward. I parked near where I had yesterday, which was nice for familiarity. I quickly grabbed my badges, electronics, and Violet, and we strode to the show floor.

"Cutting it close, are we?" Cailin asked as I pushed down the aisles to my table.

"You know it," I said with a smile.

"Where is Mr. Brian's table?" Violet asked.

"I'll take you there soon, and you can hang out with Analise for the day if you'd like. Okay?"

Violet smiled as we rounded the aisle to my booth. Today's entry process was a bit interesting. Everyone must go through metal detectors and get the wand job, and even dogs sniffed our things. Yesterday had a bit of roving security, but today was the opposite. Just an odd thing, but I notice odd things.

"Okay, can I go see Analise now?" Violet asked.

"Yes. We're going to hit the concession stand for drinks, and I'll drop you off with her after, okay?"

Violet lit up with joy. I snagged her a water and bag of Doritos and a Coke for myself. I spent the next few moments trying to reconcile how it had cost me twenty-four dollars for this.

"There she is!" Brian said as he fiddled with a tablet. "Analise just stepped away for a few, but she'll be back soon."

"She pooping?" Violet asked.

I shot a glance at her and Brian.

"Probably. Who's to say?"

Violet nodded acceptingly. I shot an awkward glance at Brian, who understood exactly who and what Violet was. It was better to answer the question with the answer she'd want than to dance around it. Otherwise we'd be here all day with a series of "why" questions.

"Cool if I leave her with you until Analise gets back?" I asked.

"Sure. I'm just getting my book trailer tablet online, but I'll watch her for a few," Brian said, poking around on his tablet.

I took a knee and hugged Violet. "Be good, and I'll see you soon. Make sure you guys check in with me and Mr. Brian if you're not at our tables."

Violet nodded. I kissed the top of her head and eyed Brian.

"I heard you," Brian confirmed. "Check in. I'll relay it to Analise when she's back."

"From pooping!" Violet added.

I smiled as I trekked toward my table and passed some usual suspects. Dan the Monster Man was set up, with his giant dragon and sasquatch inflatables in his space. He always wrote wild monster stories involving some of the craziest scenarios. Royal assembled what I could only assume with a disgusting display of viscera to advertise their newest book. I waved as I passed, thinking it would be a long day and how this one soda might not be enough.

"THE CONVENTION FLOOR IS NOW OPEN FOR EARLY ACCESS!" the voice boomed over the speakers, and a wave of about a hundred folks descended the escalators toward the show floor.

It was time, I guess. I felt like I was in *Game of Thrones*, watching the impending snow zombie army approach.

Time flew as I dealt with a few early shoppers. Before I knew it, it was 10:15, and the floor had been open for all. The crowd was intense. Bodies were everywhere. The temperature went from a crisp sixty to about ninety in the span of an hour and, had I not already adjusted to it, likely smelled of feet and armpits. After I signed a trilogy of my books, I saw a break in the crowd. I retrieved my phone to text Brian.

"She's good. They're taking a lap right now. Went to the horror tea company, since you know Analise loves her tea. And her horror."

At least I knew where they were last. As long as one of us had eyes on them, we were golden. I believed in allowing my kid to roam a bit with some freedom like we did back in the day, but I also understood the full danger of kidnappings. Analise would likely put up the biggest fight, even though she was under five feet tall. Violet was in excellent hands, with her unofficial babysitter.

I got a bit hungry and reached for my small bag that housed my bags of chips and other snacks. A mini pack of Oreos was inside, waiting for me. These things were always just a tease, giving us just enough to taste one or two cookies before shaking the crumbs into our faces like madmen.

I watched Barrios speaking with a few people holding his lizard book, and Dan the Monster Man discussing his underground worm story, based on his hand gestures.

The day would go by faster if I was nonstop talking to people. It was how it worked, you know? Keep busy and the day flies by. This twenty-minute lull was killing me, and I was eating from sheer boredom. I popped the top to my

Coke and took a giant swig, looking ceilingward as I polished off the soda.

The lights dropped out immediately. Darkness shrouded the entire convention floor. I stopped drinking and looked around. There was zero natural light in this building. Even with my reasonably superhuman night vision, I couldn't see my hand in front of my eyes. A few people screamed, others made absurd noises in the dark, but overall, I don't think anyone dared take a step.

I scanned for the faintest glow of anything—an exit sign, anything just to give me a point of reference. I reached for my cellphone in my back pocket and tapped the power button. No response. I distinctly remembered charging it last night at the hotel, alongside my tablet, which I was already immediately feeling around for. I knocked over at least two books trying to grab the tablet and felt for the power button. Nothing.

"Fucking tech, man. I charge this shit for a reason!" I said.

"Harry?" I heard Barrios's voice call out.

"Yo!" I called back.

"I can't see shit, man!" he said matter-of-factly.

It didn't require captain obvious to know we were a few moments from absolute panic from the masses. A whole minute had passed, and nobody had bothered to use the intercom or so much as scream through a bullhorn. I needed some light to find Analise and Violet. They were a few aisles from me. I just needed to get to them.

A loud metallic sound, like a moving truck door closing, erupted and filled the muffled talk and noise before stopping altogether.

Something stung my nose. The scent was putrid, like freshly cut grass and pepper. It irritated my nostrils slightly, and I immediately remembered my time in the gas chamber during basic training. The smell of the CS Gas was that of sweat and heat. I didn't know how else to describe it. My skin tingled like a mild sunburn, and I could just taste that gas. This was giving me war flashbacks from training, if that was even a thing.

"GAS! GAS! GAS!" I belted out, as if my training from nearly two decades ago had fired back up in my neurons.

Before my screaming of fire in a crowded theater sparked panic from the conventiongoers, the lights flipped on a dull, deep red. Every light. It messed with my eyes so badly, between the smoke and haze and off-red tint on the surroundings. It was disorienting.

"What the fuck is going on?" Barrios yelled, using his wizard cape as a makeshift filter for the smoke that billowed into the room. "Fire?"

I used the faint glow to navigate to his table. "Not smoke, gas."

"Like a tear gas?"

"I guess?" I shrugged, trying to keep my body hunkered low in a wasted effort to avoid the smoke.

"Your phone broke too?" Barrios asked, pressing and holding his power button in vain.

I pulled it from my back pocket and tried once more to confirm. "Yep."

Dan approached us, a tee-shirt covering his face and fogging his glasses with each breath. "This is new."

"No shit," I said, squinting through the smoke.

I needed to find Analise and Violet. Or if I located Brian first, we could team up to find our kids.

"Hey, I gotta find my kid. You mind manning the fort for a bit and keep an eye on my stuff for any looters in these trying times?" I asked Barrios and Dan, doing my best to keep my head in the game.

"Sure thing, man. If you find out anything, let us know."

I gave a subtle thumbs-up and crouched through two booths. The smoke didn't really mess with my lungs, much like we had learned about me in basic training. I remembered when Drill Sergeant Houkerman had gut checked me because I hadn't been *"coughing like the rest of the turds."* Good times, right? The most this smoke did was sting my eyes a bit and make them water.

I pushed through crowds of people huddled together. I was surprised folks weren't running and panicking yet, but I think we were all adult enough to know to stay put. Many people just sat on the floor because of the smoke, talking and trying to figure out what was happening. I hadn't gone maybe four booths from mine before the loud siren blared.

"What the entire fuck? That's going to work out my tinnitus, for sure," I said as the screaming alarm wailed throughout the building.

Five spotlights turned on, facing several large displays in the center of the building. A winch lifted them, revealing dozens of people trapped underneath. I thought that was an odd thing to see. Some sort of cloth masks covered their faces, and cloaks draped over their bodies. They wielded weapons, like baseball bats and crowbars, and some held knives and swords.

My breathing hitched as I gazed just a dozen or so feet away at the horror unfolding in front of me. One of the larger men stepped out and towered over a father gripping his young daughter. I didn't have enough time to yell, react, or say a word. Before I knew it, the masked man reared back with his club and struck the father in the skull over and over, while his daughter screamed in terror.

CHAPTER 17

"I'm a lot like you, you know? I'm empty... but I found a way to make it feel less bottomless. Pretend. You pretend the feelings are there, for the world and for the people around you. Who knows, maybe one day they will be."

— Dexter Morgan, Dexter

My heart raced. I tried my phone once more, only to find the same results. As this psychopath finished turning the grown man into a pile of paste, he focused on the man's preteen daughter. She screamed and cowered at the hulking mass of a man as he raised his bludgeon. I wanted to react, but thankfully one of the psychopath's comrades stopped him. The smaller-framed one, still masked, grabbed the larger one's forearm. My initial rough guess was that this was a woman, and something connected her to this slaughtering of a child. Then, the unimaginable happened.

The smaller killer brandished two short blades and repeatedly pierced the child through her flesh as she squealed for her father to help her. Over the sirens, I think I even heard laughter, but that could have just been my imagination. I watched, helpless, as the group marched toward the rest of the onlookers. Little by little, they smashed and slashed through the crowd. I counted at least two dozen lunatics hidden under the box.

Barrios slid behind me and tapped my arm. "What the fuck, man?" he whispered in a panicked tone.

"I know. Come on. Follow me and stay low." I pointed toward the opposing aisle. "We need to find the kids!"

We silently crept to the adjacent aisle. Barrios knew the task and kept as quiet and as low as possible. It probably helped that he donned a jet-black cloak. I wore a blood-soaked white baseball jersey, which now was a makeshift face mask to filter the smoke. We crawled from table to table amid the screams and cries for help.

"Where are we going?" Barrios asked.

I raised my hand to shush him. Movement caught my attention ahead, and I wasn't sure if it was psychos or conventiongoers. A crowd of panicked onlookers rushed past us as we took refuge under the tablecloth, witnessing a claw hammer strike the left shoulder of one of the older men in the group. He dropped to the floor, meeting my gaze. I sat in silence as one medium-built masked murderer placed a foot on the man's head and ripped the hammer from his shoulder. Based on the struggle, I knew it had been stuck in the bone.

The lifeless, open eyes of the older man stared into my soul, as if he begged me to do something, even though it was far too late. I peered out from behind the tablecloth at the assailant kicking the boots of the man he'd just bludgeoned. His back was to me, and I took my chance. Without warning Barrios, I lunged at the madman from under the table and quickly wrapped my arms around his neck.

As the murderer flailed, he smashed into a few tables. I was sure some of his friends would come to his aid. Thankfully, the siren still blared, filling the room with a deafening yet welcomed cover. I managed to lock my legs around his large waist and wrenched backward, pulling his body with mine to the floor. The man struggled to fight for air, thrashing at my arms and occasionally hitting my face. Instantly, he went limp, and I relaxed my grip and slid from underneath him

Once I could see the front of him, I noticed the claw hammer drilled straight into his ribcage, with Barrios holding the handle.

"Holy shit, man! Holy shit! What the fuck? What the fuck?" Barrios said, rocking back on his haunches, with a pale look in his eyes.

That would happen when you killed another human being. Regardless of the circumstances, it changed you. His expression ran cold. His lips relaxed, eyes widened, and nostrils flared from the anxiety. He would need a moment, but this wasn't the time.

"We have to go," I said sternly.

"Jesus, man. What the fuck?" Barrios said, running his hands through his bushy hair. "I need a fuckin' beer or a blunt. This is too much!"

I grabbed his cloak and pulled him toward me. "Get it together, man. There's a time and a place. We will find you that place, and you can unload it all. We have to go. Get your head in the game."

Barrios rose slowly and adjusted his cape to cover his face to prevent the smoke from unimpededly rushing into his lungs. He clutched the claw hammer with a death grip and slowly slid off the handle as he stood fully erect.

I gently clapped his shoulder, then squeezed slightly. "We need to move. There were more than enough of them here that we can't do this every time."

Barrios nodded as we stepped away from the body then turned and kicked the assailant's boot. He drew up the largest wad of saliva from his mouth and spat on the corpse, like a camel.

"You done?" I asked.

Barrios nodded and crouched behind some displays for cover. We slunk table to table. Smoke, sirens, screaming, and a sickening red hue that washed everything in a sea of ruby-colored light filled the air. I kept close behind Barrios as he took the lead, pushing through curtain after curtain between the tables. The half curtains were only two to three feet high, and we had to creep underneath. Nearby, we heard the screams and scuffle of a struggle. I reached for his arm to alert him to stop, but he had already halted.

"Who is that?" Barrios whispered.

I struggled to see through the haze but discerned a body shambling alongside a table, using it as a crutch to stand. As the figure drew closer, I could see it was Sawney. He looked pretty rough. Blood streaked down his shirt, as his left eye was visibly swollen. A shard of his radius bone jutted out of his left forearm.

I rose slightly, signaling to move to our area. At once, Sawney froze. His gaze met mine, a silent understanding passing between us. He slowly turned and showed a hatchet lodged just to the left of his shoulder blade. Blood gushed from the opening in large spurts. Barrios looked as if he was going to vomit at any moment. As if on cue, Sawney collapsed to the floor, pulling several items from the table with him. Barrios and I crept closer, moving one table at a time, to the end of the row. Only two tables separated us, and we had a glimmer of hope we could save him.

Sawney stood slightly once more, gripping at a tablecloth full of wood-carved dice towers for Dungeons and Dragons. The towers weighed little and instantly toppled in his direction. The towers struck the floor with an open hollow-sounding clunk, alerting anyone nearby. Before we could reach him, two retractable-baton-wielding figures stepped through the smog. No way Barrios and I could take these guys.

"Get away!" Sawney yelled, dragging his bloodied body across the floor.

It was unclear if he was yelling at his assailants or at us. It didn't matter. Within moments, the two extended their police-looking batons and mercilessly beat Sawney. We couldn't decipher much carnage, but we could hear the sound—a sucking sound as the baton pierced his skull, then pulling viscera with it. Every strike sounded wet. The sounds of bone crunching filled the air. Sawney was still moving, and we didn't know if it was his nerves still working after death or if he was, in fact, still alive and suffering.

"Stah ... stoooo ... pleee *gurgle* ..." His cries confirmed our worst thoughts as each word was gargled in throatfuls of blood.

The maniac's laughter echoed through the convention as Sawney crawled, each desperate movement met with a sickening thud of steel against bone. Eventually, his sprawling hands that clawed at any hint of the floor stopped moving.

Barrios and I sighed in relief that at least his suffering was over. The assailants pulverized his body for another few moments, then dispersed in separate directions. We could have easily been the next victims.

Barrios's hands vibrated with fear. He shook from adrenaline, anger, and a genuine terror of everything we were enduring.

"Breathe, dude. Breathe," I whispered, looking directly into his eyes.

He blinked hard and shook his head to cast off his feelings, his wild hair tossing from side to side. After a few grunts, he nodded at me to show he was ready. We slid to the end of the row and eyed the ceiling sign that marked our location. In the haze, I deciphered *800*. We'd only gone a row or two! This felt like an eternity, and miles were behind us! In reality, we'd spent five to ten minutes moved all of fifty feet. I had to admit the wind was sucked out of me.

A body lay next to the end of the table. I glanced up to see which booth was above us—a custom chopstick booth. I refocused on the body and noticed someone had jammed several chopsticks into the poor girl's eye sockets. She wore an Ice Nine Kills shirt, which was the only thing that viscera didn't cover. An eye rested just a few inches from her head, dangling from an optic nerve. Barrios and I glanced at each other in desperation.

"They plucked her fucking eye out?" Barrios cried out.

"It would seem so."

"That's fucked, man. Like, seriously fucked," Barrios said, completely abhorred.

"Let's get moving," I said to change the subject.

We glanced ahead at the rest of the building, shrouded in a mist.

"How many more to go?" Barrios asked.

"As many as it takes, I suppose."

I didn't know the answer. I just knew we needed to find the kids, a perimeter wall, and a door out of this hellscape.

CHAPTER 18

"There's a time when a man needs to fight, and a time when he needs to accept that his destiny is lost... the ship has sailed and only a fool would continue. Truth is... I've always been a fool."

— *Ed Bloom*, Big Fish

We crawled through the haze, our hands and knees landing in pools of blood, entrails, and bodies—absolute carnage and the worst nightmare I could picture to happen anywhere. I half expected Jigsaw to roll out and ask me to play a game, honestly.

"Harry?" a voice came from under a tablecloth.

Cailin poked out her head from under a table.

"How the hell are you still alive?" I asked with a grin.

"I ask myself that all the time, but more so today. Several of us hid under a table and kept as quiet as we could."

Two vendors crawled from underneath the table, who had likely dove in from the artist alley.

"What is happening?" the first girl asked.

"I don't know. A ton of crazies started taking people out, and we're doing our best to sort it out and survive," I said, eyeing Barrios.

Cailin took a deep breath, then coughed from the smoke. She glanced at Barrios, who had his cloak wrapped across his face. "Good call."

"Who are you guys?" Barrios asked.

"I'm Alisa, and this is Tara. We have a sticker and print booth just down the row. We were hiding there until our boothmate David stood up to confront these maniacs," Alisa said.

"David didn't make it. A giant gorilla of a man used a machete or something and sliced his head almost clean off, like in the movies," Tara added.

"Jesus Fucking Christ," Barrios said.

"No, it was one of the maniacs, but that's not important right now," I joked, albeit a poor one.

I got a smirk from Barrios, which I think he desperately needed.

"What's the plan, boss?" Cailin asked me.

I didn't want to be the boss, let alone the man with the plan. My plan was to find my kid, who I desperately hoped was okay, and link up with anyone I knew. After that, find a door and escape. My plan sounded extremely rational and cohesive.

"Survive." Those were the only words that came out. This single-word statement seemed to be better than laying out my twenty-stage plan for success. "We need to find Violet and Analise before doing anything. Our kids are somewhere around here."

Cailin nodded, then regarded Tara and Alisa, who seemed to be partially in agreement that we needed to move. Distant screaming and crying interrupted our meeting.

"We need to move. Let's head toward Brian's booth, which is a few aisles over. From there, we can group up and find the kids and an exit," I said.

"If we find an exit before the kids, I'm sorry, but I'm out," Tara said, with Alisa nodding in agreement.

That was fair. If nobody had to risk their lives, they shouldn't. The fewer people in here, the better. Lessen their supply of folks to bludgeon. I pointed ahead toward an open space to cross to the next aisle. The five of us slunk through each booth, sneaking from space to space behind tables and displays, careful not to make any noise.

Cailin tapped me on the back. I stopped and looked at what she was fixated on. Through the swirling smoke, I strained to see a grisly pile of bodies, limbs askew, stacked haphazardly next to a blood-spattered pillar, the stench of death heavy in the air.

"Fucking savages in this town," Cailin said.

"Who the hell are these people?" Barrios added.

I decided not to respond, to rather just keep moving. It was the best course of action. I think we would have been good to go if I hadn't slipped in the wet pool of blood. Surprisingly, slipping and falling in blood makes a lot of noise, even over the cacophony that this building had found itself dropped into. I landed right on my hip. The bad hip. The one I'd blown out in the Army all those years ago. Of course I did. I let out a soft yelp as I rolled out of the blood, trying to hobble to my feet.

The pain was too great to remain crouched. It was already a dull enough pain to do so, but I felt the adrenaline supersede that sensation. I couldn't crouch any longer and stood. With a loud pop, my hip clicked into place. I shook out the leg and the pain as best I could before glancing around. I wished I'd have looked around before standing. The man seemed delighted to see me and very clearly in an already weakened state. He grinned through his mask. This one was only a half mask, showing his teeth, which I assumed were disgusting and bathing in shitty breath. He gripped a pipe. Had he been any stronger, he'd have bent it like Superman. He was itching for a fight and almost relished in the idea of beating me to death.

I did my best to shake out my leg and assume a fighting stance. I quickly lost footing in the blood all around me, slipping and having to catch myself a few times. Carnage covered my shoes. Just behind him, I saw Tara and Alisa flee in the opposite direction and disappear into the fog.

The lumbering man took another two or three giant stomps in my direction, careful not to suffer the same fate as me in the slippery puddles. I could take a punch or two, but this guy was a fucking gorilla—a stolid oaf of a person and equipped with a blunt weapon to boot. I didn't have a chance. I squared up once more, trying to get a lower stance to adjust my center of gravity. At best, I could hope to duck under this man's lethargic swing and land a few jabs.

As I prepared for a freight train of a human to hit me, the collision never came. I closed my eyes to brace for the impact but was left standing in the aisle like a moron. Had he decided to taunt me? Had he stopped to gloat before ripping me to shreds? I slowly opened my eyes at the hulk of a human slumped down, resting on both of his knees, head tilted to one side.

"You're welcome?" Brian said, taking a sort of sarcastic bow for approval.

This surely was a sight to behold. I was more than six feet tall, and this man towered over me. Brian was almost a foot shorter than me and still had managed to disable this man. I didn't care how nor did I want to know how. I just knew he had, and now one less psychopath terrorized the floor. Little by little, the rest of the group crawled from underneath the table and slipped in the blood as they stood.

"We need to find Analise and Vi," I said, panicked.

"They're with Marissa and Callie. Come on." Brian directed me toward an area behind where he must have emerged from.

We crept toward the Marines' booth. They had their paraphernalia, like pull-up bars and recruitment pamphlets. The only thing they were missing was the Marines.

"Where'd they bug out to?" I asked.

Barrios stepped forward and pointed at a pile of tablecloths to the side. "I think we found them."

Sure enough, one camouflaged pant leg and a bloodstained boot stuck out from under the makeshift tarp.

"Probably the first to get hit, honestly," Brian suggested.

"Makes sense," I said.

We shambled toward their inflatable recruitment station and pushed through the large fabric flaps that covered the front. I heard a slow leak from the tent base. Thankfully, the rest was assembled with traditional tent pieces, and only the perimeter base and decorative parts were full of air. Behind the flaps, in the darkness, I saw figures moving.

"Daddy!" Violet called out, rushing toward me.

I embraced my daughter harder than ever. Harder than when she had been born. Harder than when a car had nearly hit her when she had been riding her bike on the sidewalk and had veered off-road. This was the most scared I'd been as a parent. Hell, it may have been the worst I'd felt as a person in general. I didn't think I'd ever felt this scared. I'd survived incoming fire from guns, rockets, and even a failed coup to overthrow a military base from the inside. That paled in comparison.

The corners of my eyes stung, mostly from the gas, but also from tears that escaped from the ducts. We were together, and that was what mattered right now. With a shared glance of understanding, we could plan our escape now. We needed to get to safety.

"What weapons do we have? Anything?" I asked.

Brian furrowed his brows and side-eyed me. "I'm not an idiot. I've been collecting what we can along the way. What do you guys have on you?"

I looked at Barrios and Cailin and noticed not one of us had brought anything.

"I had a hammer once," Barrios said.

"Good for you. Here, take this," Brian said dismissively, handing Barrios a giant meat cleaver Brian had retrieved from one assailant.

I hoped this had come from the assailants and not plucked from one of the numerous corpses of the victims.

Brian handed me a hefty pipe. "From the pull-up bar out front. It's heavy-duty shit, but they have to break it down after the event. Came off with a few pegs."

I swung the pipe in the air a handful of times to get a feel for it.

"I wish I had my gun, but they didn't even allow law enforcement to have them if they weren't actively working the event," Brian added.

I paused. "Speaking of, where is all that frigging security from this morning? All the guys doing pat-downs and cavity searches?"

"Cavity searches?" Analise interjected.

"He's kidding, but I get it. They're ghost right now," Brian answered.

I surveyed our ragtag unit. We had a few weapons and maybe two able-bodied fighters, with Barrios coming in at a close third. Nobody else seemed able to handle themselves, at least not at face value. Violet looked scared, her eyes darting around at every shadow, yet seemed more at ease now that I was here. The faint red glow barely pierced the tent walls, giving an even scarier illumination to the room. The tent wall occasionally had a shadow cast from the outside of a haunting figure.

"So, what's the plan, Dorothy?" Brian asked me. "Clicking our heels three times won't magically get us home *this* time."

I hated to lead or to be the idea guy. I just wanted to coast along. The fear in my daughter's eyes, the tremor in her small hands—a heartbreaking testament to this nightmare. I took a deep breath and closed my eyes, shaking my head to rid any cobwebs.

"Was anyone able to find a door or an exit near us?" I asked.

"I didn't pay attention to emergency exits," Cailin answered.

"Who does?" Marissa added. "Unless it's an emergency, I guess."

Callie gestured around her, stating the obvious.

"I guess you're right," Marissa continued. "There must be an exit. An office. Anything we can get in and stay safe until help arrives."

Brian and I shot each other a look of understanding. We knew help wasn't coming. This was a slaughterhouse, and we were the pigs—screams from men, women, and children instead of squealing swine.

"How many of the crazies do you think there were?" Barrios asked.

I took a moment to pause.

"Maybe a few dozen? I counted about twelve per section, and I saw three or four displays rise," Brian said.

"So, let's say fifty nut jobs with battle-axes and clubs. We're, what? A half dozen nut jobs with a few pieces of aluminum and steel?" I asked.

"Better than nothing." Brian added.

Cailin's eyes widened and her face paled. She motioned for everyone to hunker down and to be quiet, and we complied. For good reason, too, as a shadowy figure took shape near the entrance, backlit by the blood-red halogen lights burning above. We held our breaths as the curtain pushed aside, revealing a large bō staff that crept into view. I readied myself for an attack. If two of us could take one down, imagine if six or seven people dove on one.

"Holy shit, guys!" Dan the Monster Man exclaimed as he popped into view.

Our collective exhale could have inflated the Marine tent ten times over. Thank God it was a familiar face.

"We thought you were one of them," I exclaimed.

"You guys left me at my table when everything went off! I had to fend for myself," Dan grumbled.

"Sorry about that, dude. Really. We just needed to go. What happened?" Barrios asked.

Dan stepped fully inside, using the bō staff to lean on, before regaling us with his journey thus far. "Well, after the gas and psychos, one of them immediately came to our area. I didn't have time to think, so I grabbed the stone statue of the Graboid and took care of one of them."

"Took care of...?" Violet asked.

I glanced down, noticing she had connected the dots before I had to explain.

"Oh no! Not Howdy Cowboy Grabboy!" Barrios exclaimed.

"Yeah, I can get a new one made," Dan added.

Dan was so proud of a statue he had commissioned by a local stone smith of a Graboid from *Tremors*, his favorite flick. As a monster film in book form, his novels fit the bill to have a creature from his favorite movie on the table. Someone had gifted him a tiny cowboy hat, maybe for a cat, and it had been on Graboid head ever since. It was fun to see.

"Is it busted and gone?" I asked.

"In pieces. But so is the guy with the butterfly knife."

"Yikes," Brian responded.

We took a moment to collect ourselves before regrouping on our original plan.

"Let's make it to the perimeter and feel around the walls for the first door we come across," Marissa said.

I couldn't have devised a better plan. Honestly, this may sound like a lot of work but effective nonetheless.

"Which direction? East? West?" Brian asked.

"I dunno, left?" I answered.

Brian scowled in disappointment before nodding in acceptance. He pushed past everyone, taking point, through toward the curtain. We gathered behind him, prepared to push into the mystery of the unknown. Analise trailed close behind her dad, while Violet stayed glued to my side, her small hand firmly in mine. Dan and Barrios brought up the rear, and the ladies fleshed out the middle. We were en-route to uncertainty, a destination shrouded in smoke and apprehension.

CHAPTER 19

"Hey Ray, I'm going next door to complain. They're playing their stereo too loud again. Wanna come?"

— *Dr. Peter Venkman,* The Real Ghostbusters *"Knock Knock"*

The event center walls seemed miles away. Each step that took us farther from the Marines recruitment tent felt like we were lost at sea, watching our island diminish in the distance. Smoke and screams filled the atmosphere. Splats of blood specked the floor, nearly causing Barrios to slip once or twice. We covered our faces as best as we could with our clothing, keeping as low as possible.

Each table was either a pristine time capsule from right before the attack or absolutely bespattered in blood. There was no in between. We crept table by table at a pace that made it feel like an eternity. I glanced at a few of the ceiling banners obfuscated by the smoke, reading names I knew. Things Forsaken and their booth full of macabre, and Royal and their book booth, were side by side. Hell of a placement, I might add. I hoped they were okay.

We came upon a gap between aisles. By my mental math of the floorplan I barely understood, we were two aisles from the edge of the building. I only hoped we were going the short way and not the length of the building. Brian shot across the open gap, with Analise clutching the back of his shirt. I looked at Violet and gestured toward Brian. She looked both ways before crossing, making it safely to Brian, before I darted across. I glanced back at Marissa and Callie ready to bolt together, with Dan and Barrios bringing up the rear. Cailin didn't hesitate to push forward and dashed across the aisle, nearly diving under the tablecloth. The table screeched after her foot had disturbed it. We all cringed slightly, but nothing came of it.

Brian waved for Marissa and Callie to continue. They were in a discussion with Barrios and Dan, seemingly distracted. They weren't joining us. Brian clapped once, hoping to draw their attention. Marissa and Callie snapped their attention to us, then answered something Barrios had asked. The two took a breath and started to dash across the gap.

halted by a large, cloaked figure who tackled Callie like a linebacker, spilling the three onto the floor. Brian's eyes widened.

A cloaked figure, smaller than the other oafish ogres we had encountered, tackled Callie like a linebacker, spilling the three onto the floor. Brian's eyes widened. The cloaked figure wrapped their hands around Callie's throat. Marissa lay on the floor, blinking and collecting herself. Callie choked as the grip tightened around her throat. Before any of us could move, Marissa scrambled to her feet and threw her entire weight into the assailant. Upon colliding, the psychopath stumbled from Callie, who did her best to recover her oxygen in a burst of coughs, inhaling the gas-filled air.

"Fuck you! What is wrong with you?" Marissa yelled, grabbing the psychopath's hood, and drove their head onto the tile floor. After the fourth slam, the hood tore away, revealing a blonde, slender twentysomething woman. She nearly frothed at the mouth as she bucked Marissa off her. Marissa landed with a hard thud a few feet away, sliding slightly on the floor. We sprung into action.

I dove on the assailant's upper body. Brian grabbed her right leg, and even Cailin pig-piled on her. We had questions, and while this one was still kicking, we would get our answers. We moved her behind the nearest table and restrained her as best we could with a tablecloth. Marissa was a little rough for wear, and Callie clutched at her throat, trying to stifle loud coughs.

"Who the fuck are you?" Brian interrogated.

The woman smiled at him. Blood gushed down her shoulder from where her head had smashed into the tile, marked by a splat of red and missing hair on the floor nearby.

"What do you want from us?" I pressed.

Brian eyed me. "I don't think they want anything. They're not aliens or something."

"Right."

Marissa, sick of everything, reared back and slapped the blonde woman with the hardest slap I'd ever seen. "What the hell is wrong with you?"

The girl just smiled, slightly tilting her head. Her gaze trained on Callie's throat, where her hands had once wrapped around.

"It's a lost cause. This girl is bonkers," Cailin suggested.

I nodded in agreement, and a few other heads did the same. I didn't think there was any reasoning with these people. How the hell could you? A bunch of cloaked nut jobs who just started attacking random victims en-masse? We were past the point of diplomacy.

"I won't hit a woman, so just tell me what the hell you're doing here," Brian demanded.

The blonde spat a mouthful of blood at Brian, some of it spattering on Cailin.

"I'll fucking hit a bitch." Cailin balled her fist and approached the blonde psychopath, then grabbed a fistful of the woman's cloak.

"Wait! Wait," Brian said, raising his arm to stop the impending attack. "Let her talk."

The blonde emitted the brightest grin I'd ever seen since the movie *Smile*. She seemed pleased with herself, staring directly at Callie. I noticed that, for a brief second, her gaze moved from Callie to look past her in the distance. I whirled around just in time to see two hulking men, with crowbars raised, ready to strike.

Struggling to speak, I gripped Violet as we rolled slightly out of the way as the crowbar came down just past my ear. I heard the woosh. I felt the air behind it. We were kneeling, and nobody was pulling guard. What a rookie fucking mistake. You'd think I'd retain some of the basic perimeter security things I'd learned.

"Move!" a voice screamed from behind the man on the left.

A third figure stepped forward, plunging a large meat hook into one of the men's throat. With a large amount of gurgling and grasping, the first man went down, taking the hook with him. An unspoken command told us each to lunge at the other man, each of us diving for legs, waistline, or grabbing an arm. We caught the murderer by surprise as we took him down.

An animalistic instinct took over. Something tucked away in our DNA. Something primal. We each lashed out at the large man, boots and fists covering most of his body. Our rescuer even aided with a large leather-heeled boot.

"Gangbang!" Marissa yelled as we slowed our attack.

"That's not what that word means," Brian corrected.

"It's not?" Marissa inquired.

"Oh, you sweet summer child," Brian added.

The man stopped fighting back. He sputtered a few times, but overall, the fight was gone from him.

"The lady," Marissa yelled, pointing at the blonde escapee.

"On it!" Cailin barked and dove on the other assailant trying to crawl away.

The mystery rescuer removed the hook from the psychopath's neck with a wet slosh and shook it off, flinging around viscera and blood, then plunged it into the blonde's skull. Her eyes rolled into the back of her head, almost as if in a futile attempt to look at the hook before collapsing in a heap.

"Goddammit! We needed to know what they knew," Dan yelled frustratedly.

The figure pulled the hook from the skull, wiped it off on the woman's cloak, and holstered it on his belt, like he was frigging Batman.

"Ferenc?" I asked.

"I haven't been working with steel and metal for the better part of forty years to not build something worthwhile," Ferenc said with pride. "They assumed it was a foam prop. I don't work with foam. Too messy. Dig it?"

Ferenc was the prop master and carver for Things Forsaken. This guy was a wild man. Nobody knew what else he did in life or what other lives he'd led. We just knew he was a wild Hungarian man who had saved our asses. Little skulls adorned his leather vest, and his utility belt had an array of carving tools, and now a giant meat hook. In his free hand, a coffee mug. He didn't even spill a drop as he took a long sip.

"What the hell is going on here, Harry?" Ferenc asked.

"Crazy people trying to kill us? Not my circus, not my monkeys," I said.

"Dig it. Where's the little fella who was set up next to me? Royal?" Ferenc asked, pointing at the booth next to his.

"Haven't seen 'em. I hope they're okay," Brian said.

All we could do was hope. Hope and a prayer, as they said. And a meat hook. That was probably part of the quote. Hope, prayer, and meat hook. And here I was, with a lightweight bar. A meat hook was a game changer. I was sure if I'd struck that big man with the pull-up bar, he'd have laughed.

"Let's keep moving. I'm sure someone else heard that scuffle," Brian said as he pushed toward the next table.

Analise and Violet followed behind him, with the ladies quickly closing the gap. Barrios and I moved forward, filing in just behind Ferenc. I looked back at Dan, who was just staring at the carnage-filled floor.

"We need to go," I whispered to him.

Dan snapped out of it and started to walk.

I heard the sound before I saw what happened. A quick whipping noise, almost cartoonlike, as something whizzed through the air. Dan froze, dropping the bō staff.

"Dan," I yelled.

He slowly turned and fell to the floor. A large knife protruded from his back, just next to his spine.

"Go! Go!" Brian yelled.

We rushed forward into a crowd of four assailants. We were flanked. As the song says, *"Clowns to the left of me, jokers to the right. Here I am, stuck in the middle ..."* Except I'd rather deal with a clown. Unless it was a murderous clown. In that case, I guess the garden variety cloak-wearing crazy person would do.

"We're fucked," Violet said.

I didn't even want to correct her. She was right.

CHAPTER 20

"Oooh, I just know something bad is going to happen, or my name is Archibald. And it's not!"

— *Courage the Cowardly Dog*

Ferenc lunged forward, hook and a small carving blade in hand, at the crowd ahead of us, catching everyone, including us, off guard. Barrios reached back for Dan's staff, then rushed the lone knife wielder.

"Go! Get past them," Ferenc yelled as he barreled toward the horde of crazies.

For a guy with a bad back, the adrenaline made him near superhuman. The group ahead ran past the assailants as Ferenc plowed into them with monster-truck force. He yelled something in what sounded like his native Hungarian tongue before plunging what I assumed was a chisel into the man on the left's shoulder, then slammed the hook into the thigh of the middle murderer. I glanced back at Barrios, who was now out of view. We needed to keep moving. I caught up with the rest of the group.

Behind me, I heard what I could only describe as a wild animal. Maybe a bear. I peeked over my shoulder to see if Barrios was behind us, only to witness the two remaining assailants repeatedly plunge their weapons into Ferenc. The three of them collapsed onto the third one's body in a giant heap.

"Come on," Brian screamed, pointing toward what appeared to be a steel door a few rows ahead.

Our group rushed onward. We pushed through overturned tables and several bodies.

"Oh Christ! Royal!" Cailin bellowed.

Atop a pile of corpses, almost perfectly placed to taunt us all, lay Royal covered in blood and guts, from head to toe, nearly unrecognizable save for the unmistakable mustache and glasses. They were bathed in a red hue from the viscera and lights. I nearly stumbled backward.

"Not like this, man," Barrios said into the air, his cries falling on deaf ears.

"Okay. Best we can do is to get the hell out of here. We have to survive and see if we can get out and get help," I said, determined to survive this onslaught.

Brian nodded at me, as if it was the best idea anyone had concocted all day.

"Collect yourselves, because we're going through that door in a moment. I don't know what's through there, but we're fighting our way out of here, because I'm going the fuck home," Brian said, trying to give the group the push it needed to continue.

As we shook off the cobwebs, trying to steel ourselves for what lay beyond that door, something shuffled near us. We jolted alert, and a loud scream and flailing erupted from the pile of corpses.

"*Aaaaaaahhh,* fuck!" Royal screamed as they kicked an intestine from their shoes.

"Royal! Are you okay?" I asked.

Everyone seemed genuinely relieved to see another survivor among our ranks.

"I'm ... okay?" Royal asked, inspecting their body in disbelief.

"You hurt?" Marissa asked. "There's blood all over you."

"Oh. This? No, none of it is my blood," Royal said, brushing some gore off their shirt, then outstretched a sticky, blood-soaked hand for assistance.

Barrios and Callie helped Royal upright.

"What the hell happened, dude?" I asked.

Royal looked back at the small stack of bodies, scratching their scruffy chin. "Good question. Well, *this* big guy here"—Royal kicked a cloaked man's boot—"was attacking these two families." They tapped gently and politely at a little girl's sneaker with their own boot.

The mother's mouth was agape, teeth shattered and cracked by the force of a strike.

"I jumped him from behind, but it was too late for the families. Most of them were cut down by his machete right there." Royal gestured toward a machete plunged into the large assailant's sinus. "I worked on him for a while, until I got the machete free. As they say, the rest is history."

Barrios stepped forward. "That doesn't explain how you ended up where you were."

Royal glanced at the imprint left by their body. "I must have passed out. I overdid it, for sure," they said, with a smirk.

It was almost like Royal had enjoyed it. They would surely use this as inspiration for a new book. Royal was an odd duck. Then again, the fact I was unfazed by most of this, aside from the safety of everyone around me, wasn't normal either. I didn't see a difference between these lunatics and a squad downrange in the military. The goal was the same. We all needed to get back home in one piece.

"Let's go," Brian shouted and dashed for the giant metal doors.

We followed him, brandishing our weapons and makeshift bludgeons. The machete slorped from the lunatic's face as Royal retrieved their new toy. We reached the door, and I quickly instructed everyone to not stand directly in front, rather we should all peel in from against the wall—a common military tactic, called stacking. Sometimes I remembered my training. I'd tell my sergeants that I had been, in fact, paying attention, especially if I survived this ordeal.

Everyone flattened against the wall. I glanced one last time at the convention floor and at nothing but a cloud of smoke filling the air, masking the sickening red light that barely gave illumination. In the distance, I heard screaming and shouting. Tables and other large objects were being tossed, smashed, or used against someone. We needed to get out of here. I felt uneased by the number of survivors we hadn't found and the spread of victims that spilled across the show floor.

Brian put his hand on the door release. "Three. Two. One."

The door opened with a loud chunk and swung outward to reveal a large hallway with one single light in the center. This was just what we needed. A funnel to trap us on either end, with piss-poor lighting. I took point, bringing Violet in directly behind me. The rest of the group followed, and in a matter of seconds, we were closing the door behind us.

"Now what?" Cailin asked.

I crept down the hallway, putting distance from the door to the boogaloo and us as fast as possible. There must be something back here worth a damn. I knew we would have to find a loading dock or an emergency exit of sorts. Preferably without an army of guards or psychopaths blocking our exit.

The hallway smelled of must and dust. Unlike the show floor, this didn't have much of the gas in the air, and my lungs were already thanking me with each step. The one light did its best to illuminate the entire hallway, casting eerie shadows on everything that an obstacle obscured. As the hallway rounded, the darkness grew.

"We should stop for a second," I suggested.

"I think we should keep going and get the fuck out of here," Cailin protested.

I surveyed our group—a mixture of exhaustion and keyed up on adrenaline. Nothing in between.

"I'm tired, boss," Barrios wheezed out.

"Okay, John Coffee. I hear you. Take five, and then we move down this hallway. I don't want us to be so tired and worn that we are just easy pickings." I examined Brian for reassurance I was making the right call.

Those who were still full of energy or were unharmed stood watch at the ends of our area for any movement. The rest of the group slumped against walls, resting as best as they could. Violet's head lay on Analise's lap, and she was fast asleep within seconds, as was Analise. Marissa nodded off, as Callie did her best to stay awake. I knew the loss of adrenaline could sap anyone. I'd been there. Royal was a machine, just standing guard, vigilantly watching the door we had entered.

Brian remained steadfast at the farther end of the hallway. He inched closer to the edge, getting farther from our group. I did my best to monitor him. I glanced at Cailin, who held the pull-up bar.

"I'm going to see what's up ahead. Man the fort? Keep our rear covered," I said.

Cailin gave me a two-finger salute, as if from an anime, and I moved to catch up to Brian. He had already covered some serious ground. My hip was on fire, and my knee was already shifting out of place. I didn't let it stop me. I kept my war injuries in check as I closed the distance on him.

"Hey! Slow down," I whisper-yelled to him.

Brian pointed ahead of him. Following his finger, I saw a faint, pulsating glow beckoning from a nearby doorway. I glanced behind to see we'd round enough of the hallway that I'd lost sight of our entourage. I was not comfortable with how split up we'd become.

"What's in there?" I asked.

"Because I know exactly what's in there? Wonka's chocolate factory," Brian snarked.

Fair response. I had asked a stupid question. I approached the door, until a shadow moved in the space between it and the floor. Brian and I froze.

We waited to see if the shadow moved again or if our eyes were playing tricks on us. It had been a long day. Before I could reach for the door, Brian lunged for the door and thrusted it open in one swift motion, spilling blue light into the hallway. I rushed to join him as he shoulder-rammed a standing cloaked man. A second, smaller woman sat in a folding chair to the right of the door, already poised with a knife. I dove at her to stop her lunge toward Brian.

I felt a sharp, hot piercing pain in my side. The hot shifted to cold as I realized exactly what had happened. I worked to restrain the woman, slamming her to the floor. The knife bounced across the floor, leaving splatters of my blood with each metallic clank. Brian did his best to subdue the large man. I focused on the woman, wrapping my arm around her neck to slowly snuff her out. Little by little, she stopped fighting back. After I tightened my grip once more, she let out one final flop before going motionless. I loosened my grip to assist Brian, who was overshadowed by this hulk of a man by at least three feet and a hundred pounds. I raised to a knee and used my other foot to try to push upward but dropped back to the floor.

"Fuck!" I yelled as I realized the woman had stabbed me.

The fact I knew I was didn't bother me. It was the realization of the truth after the fact. I felt the blade. I felt the blood. The pain was there. My priority was to not let that woman do it again. Now that it was over, my body could focus on the more important tasks, like a knife wound.

With a grunt, I used my slippery sneakers to push myself against the nearest wall. I figured if I could use the wall to stand, I could be useful to everyone. I kicked little by little, slowly swimming my way across the floor. The blood helped lubricate my path, and before I knew it, my shoulder touched the wall. Looking upward, I found nothing above me. I wriggled myself into position to sit upright. I took my white blood-soaked-by-design button-up shirt that was my makeshift mask from around me. It quickly transformed from gas mask to tourniquet in a matter of moments. My only regret was that I wished it had sleeves. My baseball shirt button-up stretched across my abdomen, and I tied it as best as I could. The fake printed blood mixed with actual blood, blending the reality of which was which.

I pushed against the wall. Each strain felt like I would pass out. With each push, stars filled my vision. I shook off each wave of photopsia as I rose to my feet. Each time the stars filled my vision, I pressed onward. I glanced at Brian, now in an unfortunate position. A baton was inches from his neck, as the psycho hulk bore down atop him to choke him.

My vision starred up again as my body slid down hard against the wall, and my ass hit the tile floor with a thud. I tried to will myself to my feet. I thought about Violet. What if this man went down the hallway and slaughtered them? I needed to do something. Brian battled for his life, as I heard choking sounds coming from him. The ringing in my ears intensified, a deafening roar that swallowed all other noise, and then darkness fell.

CHAPTER 21

*"There are nights when the wolves
are silent and only the moon howls."*

— *George Carlin*

awoke to a sharp pressure on my side. The pain caused my eyes to well up with tears, and I winced. I did my best to pull away from the source of the pain, only to realize it was part of me. As my eyes focused, I noticed the group crowding me, as Marissa dressed my wounds with a first aid kit she had found in the room.

"What happened?" I asked, still shaking off the confusion.

"You got stabbed and passed out. Luckily you tied your shirt around yourself, otherwise you wouldn't be here anymore," Marissa answered.

Cailin kneeled toward me. "You kept saying, 'Not like this, not like this,' and 'Nobody makes me bleed my own blood,' while we were trying to stop the bleeding. Luckily I know how to sew."

Thank God we had a diverse room of people with the oddest talents. Who knew a cosplay seamstress would have the skills needed to save my life?

"I damn near passed out myself when the blood kept coming," Cailin added.

I scanned the room. "Brian? Is he...?"

Royal stepped into view, machete slung over their right shoulder. "He's good. I took care of him."

My eyes widened.

"Oh, shit. No. Not like that. I mean, like, he was getting attacked, and I took out the big guy that was on him," Royal said, panicked as they gestured toward the blood-stained machete.

I sank against the wall, relieved. My head still swirled as I tried to assess my surroundings.

"We're in some sort of security office," Brian said from across the room.

I peered through the heads that obscured my vision to see him sitting in an office chair, legs crisscrossed.

I attempted to get to my feet. Cailin and Callie assisted me into an upright position. I took a half step, wabbling like a newborn giraffe in the zoo. I took a long, deep breath, and the stitches in my side pulled taught when I exhaled quickly. Stumbling slightly over my own encumbrance, I shambled to the monitors that Brian was staring at with Barrios. I couldn't believe my eyes.

Several screens showed the carnage. Full frames of dead bodies. Women, children, and everything in between littered the aisles. Panic-stricken survivors desperately dodged their pursuers, only to be cut down. Overturned tables and chairs peppered the area, as blood smattered the aisles throughout. The imagery was blue in tone, but we could discern all the details.

"They were just sitting back here, watching the chaos?" I gestured toward the dead guy in the corner.

Barrios sat upright from resting on the table. "I guess? Bunch of dickheads, man. Sick."

Brian manipulated the cameras to pan around a bit to get the full scope of the building and of the chaos.

"There!" I pointed to the rightmost monitor. "Did you see that?"

Brian panned and centered on two, no, three individuals hiding behind a table and waving to the camera. They must have seen it moving and hoped a good Samaritan was on the other end. Until now, no one but a lunatic had been steering the ship.

"What aisle is that?" I gestured toward the bottom corner of an aisle marker sign.

The camera joystick pushed the camera into a better position. The sign slowly came into view.

"Twenty-two oh-five?" Brian shrugged in response.

"That's not far from here. We'd need to go out and hang a left. Stay low for about five aisles, and we should be right on them," Barrios added.

"You're not saying we go back into the shit, are you?" Brian asked in complete disbelief.

"I'd be down," I said.

Brian frowned, gesturing toward my bloody ribcage.

"It's just a flesh wound. I'm fine ... Probably."

Brian didn't seem amused by my answer but understood. "Take three?"

"Me, Barrios, and Royal?" I asked.

"Jesus, and leave me as one of the more able-bodied in here? Royal or Barrios, dude. Or take me and leave these guys here to guard the fort."

I hated choices, and I hated making decisions. Couldn't I just go for the ride? I thought Brian and I could easily handle the workload, but it would be better for him to stay behind. Barrios was cool and all, but was he a fighter? Royal scared me.

"I'll take Royal and come back with the survivors. Any ID on them yet?"

Brian refocused on the camera. "It's too blurry and smoky to really tell. Two guys and a lady?"

"Two kids in a trench coat?" I joked.

Barrios nearly choked on his own spit as he laughed at my ill-placed joke.

Brian spun in the chair to face the group. "Okay, here's the plan. I'm going to watch the cameras. Barrios is on door guard. The rest of you, take five, patch up, and get ready."

"Ready for what?" Callie asked, with concern palpable in her voice.

"More people. We're on a rescue mission now."

"Wait. I thought we were trying to get safe. Are we going to just sit here on our thumbs and hope the killers don't come to us?" Cailin asked.

"Yeah, won't they know to look in here?" Marissa added.

"No. Surprisingly, I think this location is off the beaten path and assumed secure. They probably didn't count on their crack team of video watchers to open the door or to get overtaken," Brian detailed.

Brian's words, as they came out, made entire frigging sense. This was unguarded. Why? Why was there not an outpouring of support by an army of psychos trying to reclaim the security room? Was this even a security room? What the hell was this place?

"Ready to go?" Royal asked, wiping the machete on their jeans.

I rotated my arms a bit and did a few squats to test my body. My knee and hip popped audibly a handful of times. No pain outside of my normal pain. "Ready."

Royal took point as we crept from the camera room. The hallway seemed darker than earlier, likely from us staring at the glowing television screens. The illumination from the single light source seemed weaker before.

"When we get outside, go immediately to the left," I said.

Royal nodded.

"From there, we go a handful of aisles up. We're looking for the aisle marker for twenty-two hundred. We need to go five rows, about halfway down the aisle."

Royal gave another confirming nod and pushed through the large metal door that separated us from the smoky crime scene beyond. Stepping through the threshold was like stepping into a different dimension. The sickly red glow poorly illuminated our way. The haze was thick. Being reintroduced to it was worse than the initial attack. Several steps into the show floor, I quickly regretted my decision.

The video room had protected us from the screams and cries through the aisles. We stepped over bodies of brutally gutted women. One woman, who covered her son, appeared to have had her jaw violently wrenched off. Some children's bodies had been mutilated, and other children had been decapitated. I turned away at the little girl who had been dismembered, her parts stacked into a sick pyramid. Any one of these could have been Violet if we didn't intervene. The cloaked ones were absolutely unhinged. This was a complete nightmare.

We crept upon aisle twenty-two hundred. Royal crouched behind a table at the end. The table, surprisingly, still had all its contents intact and untouched. I tapped Royal's shoulder to proceed. We crouched down, the machete positioned just under their chin, ready to swing at a moment's notice. Two rows crossed. Then three. We should see them any second now. Four.

An enormous figure lunged at Royal. I wanted to snap into action, but I knew if I moved too fast, too soon, I'd unravel faster than a mummy in a public restroom. My stitches would explode from my side, and I'd be absolutely useless to anyone, even more so than I was. Royal was quick enough and rolled out of the way. The bulky figure took half a step forward, and I saw my chance. I hooked his leg with my healthy arm and yanked. He crashed down with a serious thud, and Royal didn't waste a second to dive atop the assailant, poised for a kill shot.

"Stop!" the man yelled.

Through the haze and battle frenzy, we saw it was another author, B. Koscienski—Kosi, for short. He scrawled from underneath the murderous gaze of Royal, and Christine and Dennis—two other authors who shared a table with each other wherever they went—joined Kosi.

"Holy shit! We need to go," I said to all three.

"What the fuck is going on, man?" Kosi asked.

"No idea. This is the worst convention I've ever been at, that's for sure," I said.

"Second worst for me," Dennis added, still wearing his werewolf outfit—his latest promo for his comic book series. I was sure he was dying to get out of the getup.

"Really? What was the worst?" I asked.

"Well, there was this convention out in Arkansas, and I—"

"Not the time, D," Kosi interrupted.

Dennis nodded.

"Where did you two come from?" Christine asked.

"Back this way. We're safe and have a decent hiding spot. We'll show you!" Royal said excitedly.

I did a few basic stretches to ensure I could still move after jumping at Kosi. It seemed everything was intact and still together. Cailin had done a hell of a stitching job. We followed the route we had come from, staying as low as possible. Row by row, we ducked behind tables and displays. On the one hand, larger art displays were a godsend. On the other, they blocked our view of scouting around. Two more aisles and we were home free to dash toward the doors once more.

Gazing across the aisle, we saw one of the authors, Jenny, pinned under her massive signage. None of us ventured over to see if she had been killed prior to the sign collapse or if that had been the cause. She lay sprawled over a stack of books, clutching a vampire-hunting kit. My only thought was that she had tried to retrieve a stake or other sharpened object to use as a weapon but was slower on the draw than needed. All this bloodshed, and for what?

We rose slightly from our crouched position to assume more speed. Royal was nearly at a shuffling sprint by the time we hit the last table. They rounded the corner with ease and pushed forward through the haze.

Something jolted out from behind the next table. My limbs felt heavy, and words wouldn't come quickly enough to my mouth. A foot, surprisingly fast, launched itself from underneath the table and knocked Royal off balance. Their wet Chuck Taylors slipped on the polished floor as they tumbled, the squeaking sound echoing in the otherwise quiet space. With four or five desperate strides, they stumbled, gravity winning, as they fell forward with a thud. Royal did not move, as they became engulfed in the smoke.

CHAPTER 22

"Hold on to your butts."

— *Ray Arnold,* Jurassic Park

The woman emerged from under the table and struggled to stand. She stood on her own cloak, almost yanking her back to the floor. I made a mad dash for Royal, only to notice that they'd impaled themself on their own machete. It looked quick, and they hadn't suffered. The woman stood to her feet, producing two daggers. I felt like I'd seen her before. Was she the child stabber from earlier?

"Look out," Kosi yelled, charging toward the woman, and hit her with the full force of his weight.

They crashed hard through a wooden table and slammed to the floor. It looked like a wrestling scene. We were just missing the colorful commentary.

"Good gawd!" Dennis and Christine yelled.

Well, there it was. Ask and you shall receive, right? Kosi slowly rose to his feet. As he stood upright, his white clown jersey filled with spots of red. He dropped to a knee.

"Kosi!" Dennis yelled as he and Christine rushed to him.

"I'm fine. I'm fine. You should see the other guy," Kosi joked.

The four of us beheld the absolute pancaked psycho laying in the chaos of splintered wood and viscera.

"Other woman. Sorry." Kosi laughed as we assisted him to his feet.

The red pooled faster and harder than ever.

Kosi eyed two large daggers near the body. "I think she got me a few times." He collapsed slightly once more.

"We have first aid where we are holed up. Let's get him back there," I commanded.

Christine and Dennis hoisted Kosi onto their shoulders, supporting his weight. I tried to regain my bearings to correct our course. It was unfortunate about Royal. They had been a talented author and a good person. We needed someone like them in this calamity. I slowly reached for the machete handle, the blade wedged into Royal's shoulder blade, piercing the neck in the process. I tightened my grip on the handle, ready to give it a good pull.

"Look out!"

I pulled the machete from Royal. Without thinking, I swung blindly behind me, but a wet, slicing sound stopped my momentum. I glanced back at what I had swung at and saw a cloaked man looking as surprised as I was, clutching at his throat. I had hit my mark, that was for sure. The man clawed at the blade as he sank to the floor.

I withdrew the blade, staring in him eyes. "For Royal and everyone else, you fucks!"

I must have ruptured a stitch as I swung the blade at the other side of the man's neck, severing his spinal column. His head hit the floor and rolled with a shocked expression toward Christine. My ribs screamed with pain.

"Holy shit!" Christine yelled. Blood spurt from his neck, splashing her glasses. She turned and vomited instantly.

"Can we be a little more tact in our cold-blooded murders?" Kosi asked, becoming very pale. His white Clown Killer jersey, now a shade of maroon, appeared wet and heavy.

"You better make it, or I'll kill you!" Christine commanded Kosi.

He smiled at the notion. "You don't have the balls."

Christine grinned as she and Dennis helped him to his feet. We didn't need another delay. We needed first aid. The familiar clammy weight against my skin confirmed it; my side was wet again. I had absolutely torn a stitch or two. I hadn't made it this far just to bleed out on the floor.

"This way!" I yelled, pushing forward.

My hip and ribs ached. Everything was on fire. Everything screamed with pain. I tried to muster whatever adrenaline still floated around in my body to push forward and slammed into the large metal door that separated me from salvation. I reached for the door release and slid into the doorway, thrust into darkness. The single hallway light, still a poor source of illumination, beamed strong just around the bend.

"Inside! Now!" I commanded, holding the door open.

Christine slid inside, pulling Kosi inside with her. Dennis stopped dead in his tracks.

"Come on!" I yelled.

"Go. I'll stop these two," Dennis said.

I glanced past him to see two cloaked crazies creeping up on us. One with a baseball bat, the other with a switchblade that he flipped around dramatically.

"Hey!" I yelled to Dennis.

He looked back as I produced the machete.

I put the handle into his hand. "Don't die."

"We'll see. Get them out of here." Dennis eyed Kosi and Christine.

"Oh, fuck you, man. You don't get to be a damn hero. If you die, I'll give you such a hard time," Kosi joked, his words getting a little wet with blood.

Dennis saluted him and faced his offenders.

We closed the door behind us and moved forward. The door did well to muffle and drown out the sounds of the carnage just beyond.

"This way. Follow the light to the open door," I ordered.

Christine and I did our best to keep Kosi upright. He'd lost a lot of blood. My clothing was getting wet and sticky with his blood. Part of that could have been my own. We rounded the corner past the single white light and saw the open door. Salvation lay just ahead.

"We need medical!" I yelled.

Cailin stepped from the office. "Oh, shit!"

She quickly went back inside and returned with Brian and Barrios. The two of them assisted Christine and me inside the screen room. We placed Brian against the very same wall I had rested against not long ago.

"Okay, doc. How am I doing?" Kosi asked.

Cailin removed the clown jersey from Kosi. "Jesus Christ," she said as she stood up.

"What?" I asked, pressing gauze against my own reopened wound.

"Well, he's holier than a nun in church at the Vatican, that's for sure," Cailin added.

"I went for a Hail Mary!" Kosi added, slightly choking on the words.

I inspected him as Cailin removed the jersey, which let so much light show through the holes. If his body was thinner, he'd have done the same. At least two dozen knife cuts graffitied his front alone. His arms and shoulders had cuts and stabs peppered throughout.

"It's fine. Save the supplies. I kicked some ass today. I'll just sit here and sing some showtunes. Does anyone know the words to 'Bright Side'?" Kosi mumbled the words to "Bright Side" by Eric Idle. Each line delivered becoming more muddled and wetter than the last. With every line, his smile widened, a silent acknowledgment of the words he spoke. "Life's a piece of shit, when you look at it," Kosi sputtered out with a laugh.

When he hit the chorus, several of us hummed or lightly sang along. I even heard Brian whistle in between. Eventually, we lost a singer in our entourage. He relaxed slightly where he sat.

"B. Kosi, everyone. Master of Shenanigans until the very end," Christine added through tears.

Marissa and Callie rushed to comfort her. I felt a stinging in the corners of my eyes, too.

Brian approached me. "I know now isn't the time for more salt in the wound." He espied my red-soaked side.

"Poor choice of words, I get it. I found something while you were gone."

A slow, intrigued raise of my eyebrow hinted at my curiosity.

"So, I was perusing around on the computer and camera system when I noticed something a bit off. I clicked the icon and saw something."

"What? What did you see?" I asked, dabbing gauze on my wound.

Brian took a deep breath and released a large, disappointed sigh. "They're recording and transmitting all this camera footage. All of it. Every second of it."

I dropped the blood-soaked gauze to the floor. I shot a look to the far corner at Analise and Violet, fast asleep in a nest of security crew jackets. "You're fucking kidding me. All of it?" I hissed.

"Every. Second."

CHAPTER 23

"Life is an endless series of trainwrecks with only brief, commercial-like breaks of happiness."

—   Ryan Reynolds as Wade Wilson, Deadpool

I couldn't believe my eyes. An app was transmitting the footage to somewhere off-site. What the fuck was this? All at once, it hit me.

"You know how his movies are super fucked up and realistic looking?" I asked.

"Whose?" Brian asked.

"Mayfield!"

Barrios shuffled over to join the discussion. "His movies *did* always look too intense and real."

"Fucking right! It does make sense," Brian added, standing to his feet from the office chair.

All the gears just turned. Every puzzle piece clicked. This was just another installment in the Mayfield Mayhem films. The offices we watched? Real people. The subway station? A real, locked-down subway station with a crazed killer. This was just the latest installment. We were the actors screaming for help now.

"Did you stop the transmission?" I asked.

"Obviously," Brian said. "Why the hell would I let him finish his film?"

I nodded. That was a fair point, and a dumb question to ask.

"What now, then?" Barrios asked.

Everyone crowded near us, as if they knew we needed to take a next step.

"Okay, let's look at the facts," Brian started. "These movies are just that. Films that are using real people and real carnage. Is it a safe bet that nobody survives?"

I looked at Barrios and Cailin.

"Gods," Cailin added.

"I don't think they're here with us now," Barrios said to her.

Everyone slumped a bit, losing the wind in their sails, if there had even been any to start with. I just wanted to be off this ride. The expressionless masks everyone wore told the whole story. We were just over the entire ordeal. How much longer would we have to battle psychopaths? Was this our lives? Where was the rest of the world?

"What now?" Callie asked.

I grunted as I stood fully to my feet. "What now, folks?"

Brian wiped at his face with both hands, pulling down hard. "FUUUUUUUUCCCCCCCKKKK! I don't know."

Cailin moved toward the door. Everyone's gaze followed her as she stopped at the threshold to peek down both sides of the hallway. "I'm getting the fuck out of here if it kills me," she said as she stepped through the doorway.

This was it. The final push, as they say. We have only two options ahead of us—either sit pretty and hope someone rescued us or let the crazies try to slaughter us in this room. At least we'd see them coming on camera, I suppose. Option B seemed a little more open-ended. We would just rush through their ranks, cutting them down with rebar, lead pipes, and machetes, until nothing remained to fight back. We could work on the doors and get the fuck out of this hellscape.

Our second option seemed to be the unspoken choice, as Christine approached the door to join Cailin. Barrios and Marissa slowly shuffled to the doorway. I furrowed my brows at Brian.

"What? Is this the last stand? Us or them?" Brian asked.

"I guess so. We go out swinging, or we die trying," I answered, staggering toward the door.

Brian woke up Violet and Analise, who groggily clung to his side. Everyone traversed the dark hallway and rounded the bend. The one light spilled an eerie hue over us as we passed underneath it—the false hope of a normal light in the sea of red. We were about to enter the gates of hell. There was just a steel security door right ahead of us.

"Ready?" Barrios asked, hand on the door handle.

"No, but let's do it anyway," I said.

The door squealed open, crimson light shrouding everyone's faces. Swirls of gas and smoke still filled the room's air, and the droning alarm buzzed in between the occasional scream. Barrios raised his cloak to mask his face to breathe. Everyone fashioned their shirts or other clothing accessories into makeshift gas masks.

I surveyed my white blood-printed jersey, now soaked with my own blood. "Fuck it," I said, pushing past everyone.

I stumbled into the abyss. The show floor looked absolutely alien to me. The aisles adorned with crochet crafts, creepy macabre art, and wood-worked creations resembled a nightmare on steroids. I stepped forward to get my bearings. One by one, everyone peeled from the room and surrounded me. Not a soul was in our area. No one alive, that is.

"If we go straight across this way and hang a right, we should end up near the escalators and elevators, right?" Cailin asked.

"You act like I even knew where I was at this event?" I joked.

"Fair."

"Come on," Marissa commanded as she pushed past all of us, Christine and Callie in tow. Barrios followed close behind.

I shrugged at Brian as we moved forward. We kept our kids behind us to keep them safe. It was easier for me to navigate the killing floor when they weren't with us. Now I had to watch every step. Barrios and Cailin took the lead, navigating everyone through the carnage. The floor was a mix of red light and viscera. It was hard to tell what was blood and what was light. Everything was like a bad dream on drugs.

"This way," Barrios ordered, navigating around a giant display of Krampus merchandise.

I almost thought about what had happened to the vendors. I assumed they were in the mix of the bodies we stepped around. It proved hard to tell the vendors from the attendees. Families lie broken all around us. Savagery at its peak.

"Jesus Christ, don't look. Oh my gods!" Cailin covered her face and drifted to the right.

As Brian and I came up on it, I instantly shielded Vi's face. Someone had beaten an attendee's service animal to death. Its harness was filled with veteran emblems and a few giant patches that read, PET ME! I'M FRIENDLY! and MY NAME IS DOUGLAS! I'M A GOOD BOY, littered its harness.

"I never kill fucking animals in my books for this reason," I said as we pushed past the poor labrador—or what was left of it.

Ahead was one of the areas where the psychos had started this boogaloo. Large boxes that had originally been designed as set pieces for a haunted house movie hung overhead. A photo-op-turned-murderer storage, I supposed. This wasn't near our booths, but it looked to be more of the same. A crowd of people standing in horror, being struck down one by one, before realizing it wasn't part of the show. Fight or flight kicking in far too late for far too many.

"This way," Barrios called out.

We whipped to the right and rounded another corner also devoid of the psychos. I wondered where they'd all gone to. I wish I hadn't thought of it.

"Fuck!" Callie yelled out.

I looked ahead at wall of culty crazies—hoods on, weapons at the ready—standing silently motionless and menacing. Talk about dramatic.

"What the fuck do you want? Let us go!" Cailin screamed.

I glanced just past them. The exit *had* to be up ahead. I knew it did. Why else would they block this way?

"Rush them?" Brian asked.

"All forty of them?" I replied with a bit of snark.

"Fair point."

"What now?" Barrios called back to us.

"Daddy, I'm so scared," Violet said, tears staining her cheeks.

Analise latched hard onto Brian as we surveyed the attackers.

"There!" Christine pointed to our right.

Another wave of psychos stood at the end of the aisle, observing us—waiting for something. Were they waiting for instructions? It was like the ref at a wrestling match had lost his headset communication and didn't know whether to call the match or continue.

"I bet those ding-dongs in the screening room were calling the shots. They relayed orders," Brian said.

"No shit?" Barrios raised an eyebrow in surprise.

"They won't kill us because they don't know if they *should* kill us," Christine added.

Those were the wrong words. As if on cue, the two squads of killers marched in our direction. Blades brandished occasionally, catching the light, glinting with sharpness.

"Fuck!" Cailin said, backing into the rest of us.

I gripped my crying daughter hard. This was it. Regardless of how hurt I was or how tired, I'd exercise my cliché use of *over my dead body.*

CHAPTER 24

"How could this be for the greater good?"

— *Simon Pegg as Nicholas Angel,*
Hot Fuzz

"**O**N THE GROUND! ON THE GROUND!" a voice shouted from the fog.

With a loud thump, the lights flipped to their regular incandescent white. My eyes burned, and I shielded mine and Violet's faces from the blinding light. Gunfire immediately erupted. Screaming filled the air, much like it had for this entire ordeal. After a few moments, the firefight ceased. I attempted to adjust my vision to the new light. My eyes watered with each passing second.

"What is happening now?" Cailin screamed.

We were a whole new level of terrified. We didn't know what was going on, and this was new. These guys had guns. I focused my eyes enough to see through the haze that they appeared to be SWAT or some sort of police force. Was this part of the stupid movie? Were they more insane actors?

Barrios pushed toward our potential rescuers.

"ANOTHER ONE! ENGAGE!" one of them ordered.

Red laser lights trained on Barrios. None of us could speak up fast enough as echoing blasts from their rifles filled the cavernous convention center. Barrios stood in place, reacting to each shot that pierced his body. After about another dozen shots, they stopped. Barrios stood still, staring at the crowd, before slowly turning to face us. The machete in his left hand dropped to the floor. I don't even think he remembered he was holding it.

"Fuck! The cloak," I yelled.

"POLICE! SHOW US YOUR HANDS!" one screamed as they approached us with the rifle aimed at Cailin.

We did our best to raise our hands and kneel. Barrios looked at everything, then collapsed in a giant heap on himself while grinning, which will forever haunt me.

"Are there anymore?" the first rescuer asked.

"Survivors or killers?" Brian replied.

"Either," the lead rescuer screamed back.

"We're here. That's all we know," I retorted.

Violet wailed louder than ever before. Everything was so sudden and upsetting. The initial strike team pushed past us and fanned out into the rest of the building. The occasional gunshot or two resounded as paramedics escorted us from the building. I sat at the edge of an ambulance as one responder triaged my stab wound, among other injuries. They inspected Violet about a thousand times. Each time they shifted their focus from her and to worry about me, I'd insist they handled her.

The outside air was so fresh it was painful. Inner city smog and pollution were nothing compared to the cloud of death that hung in that building. I glanced at the convention center and noticed a familiar face sprinting toward us.

"Oh, my God! You guys!" Audrey said, gripping both me and Violet in an embrace.

I winced in pain but pushed through it.

"They said on the news that you guys were in danger. I left work and rushed here as soon as I could," she rattled off.

"The news?" I asked, feeling dizzy.

"It was everywhere. Customers were coming in and telling us about it," Audrey added.

I became nauseated. The world spun, and I eventually found myself reaching for the ambulance door. Everything got dark, fast.

DAYS LATER

> *"Since it began, who have you killed? You wouldn't be alive now, if you hadn't killed somebody."*
>
> — *Major Henry West*, 28 Days Later

CHAPTER 25

*"Anyone feel like dying today?
Step forward. I'll fight until my heart
stops!"*

— Victor, Suikoden

came to, hearing machines beeping and PA announcements. Drew Carrey was hosting *The Price is Right* on the small television to the right of me. I darted my gaze around to see that I was in a hospital room.

"You're awake!" Audrey exclaimed. "You were in and out for the past two days. The doctors said you were hurt and exhausted."

I nodded slightly. I tried to sit upright, feeling the pressure on my rib cage. A sharp, searing pain shot through me, making me recoil and instinctively grab the blankets to figure out what had happened.

"They had to remove a piece of a knife from you and stitched you up. You'll need antibiotics for a bit, but otherwise you'll survive," Audrey said.

I focused on the television. Someone was about to bid one dollar higher than the other.

"Mr. Carpenter. Feeling better, are we?" a voice said from the other side of the room.

I rolled my head to see a doctor reading my information on a computer screen. I'd never seen this doctor nor had I been in this hospital before. "Where am I?"

The doctor looked up from my charts. "In excellent hands. I'm very sorry for happened to you and your friends." He rose, holding a clipboard, and approached my bed. "Just a few routine things. What is your pain level?"

"The usual," I said.

He frowned at my answer but marked down a response. "I have a referral, paid for by the city, to speak to a grief counselor. This person should be able to help you process the trauma you endured."

Grief counseling. I don't want to process this mess; I want to go home and see my cat and resume my normal life with my family.

"Judging by the look on your face, this isn't favorable. You're required to go to one. After that, you're free to attend up to ten prepaid sessions. I've given your wife the number to schedule the appointment."

Audrey lovingly squeezed my hand.

"You'll be free to go this evening, if all goes well. We're waiting for a few more tests. Other than discomfort, is anything severely bothering you? Headache? Nausea? Anything we should know?"

"Nothing out of the ordinary, or what I'd expect after being dragged through hell."

This guy had no idea. I just wanted to leave. The sooner they could have me piss in a cup, the better. Whatever they were planning to test, I wanted it over with. The doctor nodded, with a smile, and placed my charts near the computer, then exited.

I returned to watch *The Price is Right*. I bet the dishwasher was at least $1,400. It was a good one.

EPILOGUE

I watched a few YouTube videos and read some articles while resting on the sofa at home. Pigley lay by my legs, grunting and purring as always. According to the articles, the whole ordeal only spanned three and a half hours. It had taken them that long to figure out what was going on, respond, and breach. Thank God no one was in danger, right? Between response time and overall clumsiness and confusion, we were in that hellscape far longer than ever desired.

They found Dennis, barely alive, after the second sweep of the building. They airlifted him to a nearby town, where they expected him to recover from his multiple lacerations and bruised skull. Overall, they considered him lucky. I didn't even want to know what they'd consider unlucky. I was glad to read some positive news about the event, even if it was minor.

The news reports still trickled in, with varying claims. One station said over 800 deaths, while another had a body count at 1,700. If I was a betting man, it would be somewhere in between. In any case, they listed hundreds of men, women, and children. Elderly to infant, nobody had been spared. Those who had survived were separated from loved ones or had lost someone close to them. So much loss for what? What was the fucking point? I felt myself getting angry, which would flare up my injuries.

Pigley looked up at me as I readjusted myself. I scrolled through more links and articles. In three hours, these goons had easily decimated half of the attendee list. Benjamin Parker was set to stand trial once they found him. The police had issued multiple warrants for his arrest, but a growing number of people had a suspicion that he hadn't survived the ordeal either. Parker was a great event runner, and I'd go as far to say that he had nothing to do with this chaos and had either been held hostage or was dead. Regardless of his fate, I believe he was innocent of everything. He had been just trying to run a wonderful event and take it to the next level.

We attended a mass funeral for those we lost at the event the following month. The city had organized a charity ball to support those affected. It was a sympathetic gesture, but money and a plaque do not bring loved ones back. I had been lucky enough to escape with Violet. Others, not so much.

Barrios's partner was among the grieving party. The mayor presented them with a key to the city and unveiled Barrios's name on the fancy wall that now adorned the convention center's interior. The last thing I'd want was for my resting place to be where someone had killed me. Then again, I guess the same could be said if we had to mass bury a ton of people at a crash site. Typically, a memorial or a marker identified the area to signify the event. Never forget 9/11 and all that, right? I guess this was more of the same.

During the ceremony, an older man spoke at the podium about loss and grief, then offered a poem. "Butterflies born of the cocoons woven, the soul—" He stopped, seemingly choked up. "The soul ... You know what? Wherever Mayfield is, I hope he rots in hell! I hope they pull him apart with horses and feed his carcass to the local hungry wolves. I hope—"

The ushers quickly pulled him off stage. He continued his rant until he was out of earshot.

He had brought up a grand point. The authorities hadn't caught Mayfield yet. The Supreme Court had held a hearing a few weeks ago about his case. They had pulled every one of his films into question. The court had determined that the films, much like his most recent endeavor, had been all footage from actual crimes against humanity. I was set to testify, after they had pushed the hearing out another several months.

My lawyers tell me that it would be good to tell my story. The therapist had agreed during my mandatory therapy appointment. Therapy wasn't my way of coping; I preferred other methods to process my feelings, like writing crime stories and/or horror tales. That was my therapy. For me to sit and blab about my feelings would be a lost cause. If only I had the energy and brainpower to write something now.

Mayfield never surfaced. Presently, my attorney stated they were pushing for the death penalty, and Mayfield would be tried for hundreds and hundreds of crimes. This Hitler-esque mass murderer was a borderline war criminal, and the courts would probably treat him as such. The quantity and gravity of the kills had been a dividing factor. Die-hard Mayfieldians had taken to 4Chan and other socials to express their loyalty. One went so far as to say he'd make even better movies than his hero.

Just a week and a half ago after this writing, we finally laid our friends to rest in a more intimate ceremony. Barrios had an outpouring of fans surrounding the outside of the funeral home. A lot of them wore shirts with his characters on them. Several appeared to have fashioned gold jewelry like the chief deity wears in his story. If he only knew how many people were into his story in life.

The most recent monster movie gave Dan the Monster Man a posthumous credit. It dealt with dragons and a group of mages destined to fight them with an ancient power, as it held the ability to control minds. At the very end, a stinger appeared as the screen faded to black: *For Dan, our Monster Man and friend.* Apparently, he had partially written the movie in its early stages.

Jenny's cohorts gave her a celebration of life at Anne Rice's home. Odd, I know. Her influence in the current vampire world was nearly as impactful as Rice in her day, and it seemed only fitting. According to the Instagram post, several attendees dressed as her main characters, celebrating in her honor until the sun rose.

Ferenc's fans immortalized him at several Renaissance fairs. They jousted in his honor, and one wood carver even sculpted a likeness of him to put in the major thoroughfare to get to the arena. Ferenc had been a weaponsmith and an expert carver, so it was only fitting. The

King held a memorium, and the trumpets played as the crowd cheered with thunderous "Huzzah" and "Adieux." For as odd a ceremony as it was, it was beautiful. Violet enjoyed eating a giant turkey leg that afternoon.

Others we knew were kept quiet or remained so private that we weren't even invited. I hoped their loved ones could manage. I didn't know what Audrey would do without me. Probably be sad for a few moments, then move on. She hated that joke. The real question would be, "What would Pigley do?"

I stared at him by my feet as he grunted once more. For a fat black cat, he sure was a damn potbelly pig. I found comfort in scrolling mindlessly through my phone and relaxing with the fat boy, drooling on himself and as happy as he could be. I scrolled through more Facebook feed before an incoming call from Brian interrupted me.

"What's up, man? How are you holding up?" Brian asked.

I looked at my crutch. "I've been worse, I guess."

There was a brief pause. "I was just seeing how you were doing. How's my favorite troublemaker?"

"Vi? She's out right now with her mom. They went to some school function. I've been home all alone with the cat."

"Poor you. Getting out of the house at all?"

"Here and there. I was actually going to go to the crepe shop to see if I could put some words into a book."

"You sure you won't just sit there and play on Facebook?" Brian asked.

"If I wanted to do that, I'd stay here on the couch. You're right though; I should get outside a bit more."

Brian hesitated. "I keep thinking about everything. Have you checked on everyone else?"

"No. I lost touch with Cailin. She's gone completely dark. No social media and not answering my emails either."

"Jeez. Callie and Marissa have been bouncing back. I was worried for a bit, but they're pretty resilient. Copious amounts of therapy will help with that, though." Brian released a deep sigh. "I'll let you get back to it. I was actually taking a quick break and wanted to check on you. Give me a call if you need anything, man."

"I appreciate that. Same with you."

The phone disconnected. I checked the time and saw it was still pretty early in the day. Barely noon. I apologized profusely to Pigley and stole my legs from under his chin. I tossed my laptop and charger into my bag and looked at the door. It had been weeks since I'd resumed my daily routines. Even now, I barely cut the grass, went shopping, or socialized. I hadn't seen Paul since the incident, and we were due to talk wrestling.

The crepe shop was somewhat busy, but my usual spot was available. I set down my bag and fired up my laptop while Paul took orders. I grabbed a can of Coke in the meantime and logged into my computer.

"There he is!" Paul said from behind a crowd of patrons. "I've been wanting to talk to you."

I stared at my desktop wallpaper. One by one, the customers got their orders, while Paul and James tag-teamed the service counter. Irina moved crepes faster than anyone. The family business was booming, even for a Tuesday.

Paul sat across from me at the table, placing my usual crepe order in front of me. "I heard all about what happened, man. That shit is wild."

I nodded.

"I just keep thinking about what I'd be capable of doing if I had been in that situation. I almost thought about attending the con just to pop in and bug you. Nightmares Unbound was really a nightmare, wasn't it?"

I took a sip from my soda can. "It was unlike anything I'd ever experienced, that's for sure."

Paul leaned forward and spoke softly. "You don't have to tell me, but how many people did you, *you know...*"

I looked at him dead in the eyes and gave the response I'd given ever since returning home from Iraq. "All that needed to go."

Paul nodded in agreement. "So, have you been following WWE? Holy shit, Triple H is on fire these days. I'm just excited to see how they do things at the PPV this weekend."

Without missing a beat, Paul discussed the regular trappings of life—wrestling, videogames, movies, and my thoughts on the state of the world. Nothing had changed. Just like when I had gone to war and back. Everyone else had stayed the same. I guess the Earth remained still, and I was still in orbit.

It was funny how surviving a traumatic moment could be like that. The world wasn't necessarily on pause, but it felt like it. Everyone else just moved at a normal pace, and I'd been fast-forwarded through growth at an alarming rate. I recalled from before I had gone to basic training to the day when I had returned home, and it wasn't too far off from this experience.

Paul went to help a few more customers until the herd died down, then quickly dashed to my table to bend my ear once more. My computer just sat on the desktop screen, slowly draining itself of battery life, while I did nothing. I stared through the large window at the passersby.

"It's such a wild story, dude. Like, for real. I'd watch it if it was a movie. No offense," Paul joked.

Something sparked.

I manhandled my wireless mouse, quickly ensured I was connected to the restaurant's Wi-Fi, and launched Microsoft Word. Letter by letter, sentence by sentence, it poured out. I remembered some details more than others. Moments from the ordeal were etched into my mind. Barrios's unfortunate situation was the most vivid, yet I remembered so little. I think the kid's expression when the killers first emerged will live with me the longest.

As Paul yammered on about wrestling for a minute, I glanced up, only for a second.

He stopped talking about the over-the-top cage match from Monday and met my gaze. "What? You okay?"

"Dude. I know what my next book will be."

AUTHOR'S NOTE

I hope you enjoyed the ride we just went through. There were several deaths that I had to think about, and others that were a no-brainer, or ones that the author absolutely suggested themselves! Fun fact about this book, though: I struggled to produce anything (if you're looking at the timeline of publications, I released *FUBAR 3* in the same year as this novel but had written that one three years ago), save for the already written short stories I slapped together into a collection. Aside from that, nothing. I had written nothing since *Chemical Burns* (which I wrote *FUBAR 3* during most of the downtime of that book's creation.)

The plan was to write something wild. I had a few book ideas in the chutes but nothing that motivated me to get to the end of the book. I was sitting in Irina's Crepes, talking to Paul, and presented him with the idea. Yes, Paul is real, and so is the crepe shop. They have even named a crepe after me! It's got bacon and cheese and will probably be the death of me.

I would bring up the ideas and scenes to Paul, who loves the same type of gross horror I watch. He's always discussing B-movies with me, and we have a love for this stuff. I remember running the first scene, where the killers take out the dad and ultimately kill the kid, by Paul. It's a visceral scene. Paul cringed at the uttering of the scene. I knew I was on to something.

My favorite part about writing this has been the fact that I, myself, run a horror convention. FrightReads Book Festival has been going strong for five years now! Whenever I told people I was writing a book where a horror convention killed its attendees, I loved following it up with, "Oh, you should come to FrightReads!" It got a few raised eyebrows.

I used some of that knowledge in my design of the show floor and posters and promotional work for the fictional event. My biggest obstacle was that I didn't want to discuss the celebs, special guests, and other real-world bigger deals. I also heavily fictionalized my success. That's really the only difference between me and this book version of me. Also, I don't have a kid. Beyond that, nothing is really all that different.

Drawing on my real-world military experience, I described the intense physical and emotional challenges I had faced. The pungent smell of gas, combined with the eerie, low-level red tactical lighting, evoked a specific atmosphere inspired by numerous sources. While my killers lacked projectile weapons, they more than compensated with creatively thrown knives and axes, the glint of steel a terrifying sight. Nobody possessed a firearm, a crossbow, or any other ranged weapon. I was tempted to include a crossbow, remembering how brutally effective they were used in movies—a silent, swift death.

The end scene was more shocking because it was the first time the characters heard gunshots for the entire story. I wanted it to be something so alien in this world, shrouded in gas and darkness. What else would shake things up? The local law enforcement just firing rounds into the bad guys, right? Everything was exciting and fun for me. I wanted to keep scenes that even I went, "Oh, no shit?" when I reread them. Between Royal wielding a machete like a lunatic and Barrios going ham on people, I just entertained myself with some of the farfetched scenarios that I laid out.

In the end, I hope you had a good time! As promised in the intro, I have listed below the authors and creatives who took part in this carnage. Please check out some of their books, if you could. Yes, Sawney *does* have a book involving a space cat. Thanks again, and I'll see you at the NEXT CONVENTION! Too soon?

AUTHOR & CREATIVES LIST AND LINKS

BRIAN PAONE:
https://www.brianpaone.com/

J.A. BARRIOS:
 https://linktr.ee/ja_barrios

DAN JONES:
https://creatureauthor.com/

SAWNEY HATTON:
www.sawneyhatton.com

MARISSA D'ANGELO:
www.mystywrites.com/

CALLIE RAE SUTTON:
https://linktr.ee/crs13

REDTAIL STUDIOS:
https://linktr.ee/RedtailStudios

THINGS FORSAKEN:
http://www.thingsforsaken.com/

HIVE HEAD STUDIOS:
https://www.hiveheadstudios.com/

ROYAL POFF:
https://linktr.ee/robertroyalpoff

FORTRESS PUBLISHING INC:
https://www.fortresspublishinginc.com/

JENNY ALLEN:
https://www.jennyallenbooks.com/

Please take some time to check out all their wonderful books and art! I hope you enjoyed everyone in the story!